THE WOLF'S QUEST: ISA'S ADVENTURE BEGINS

THE WOLF'S TALES
BOOK ONE

MARK GREATHOUSE

WISE WOLF
BOOKS

The Wolf's Quest: Isa's Adventure Begins
Paperback Edition
Copyright © 2026 by Mark Greathouse

WISE WOLF BOOKS
An Imprint of Wolfpack Publishing
1707 E. Diana Street
Tampa, FL 33610

wisewolfbooks.com

Paperback ISBN 978-1-968733-31-5
eBook ISBN 978-1-968733-30-8

Also by Mark Greathouse

The Frontier Chronicles

Perilous Trails: Jack's Adventure Begins

Wyoming Calls: Jack's Risky Quest

Longhorns North: Jack's Great Trail Drive

Warpath: Jack's Faith is Tested

Hunter Vs. Hunted: Jack's Great Frontier Challenge

Freedom Drovers: Jack's Awesome Crusade

A Poison Spreads: Jack Seeks the Antidote

Darkness Looms: Jack Faces War

The Tumbleweed Sagas

Nueces Justice

Nueces Reprise

Nueces Deceit

Nueces Blood

Nueces Grit

Nueces Truth

Nueces Legend

The Tumbleweed Sagas - Junior's Story

Lone Star Vigilante

Guns on the Guadalupe

Railroad to Perdition

Nicholas Dunn: The Making of a Texas Legend (A Western Adventure)

Dedicated with love to my wife Carolyn, our two sons, Mike and Matt.

Do not repay evil with evil or insult with insult. On the contrary, repay evil with blessing, because to this you were called so that you may inherit a blessing.
  —1 Peter 3:9

Do not repay anyone evil for evil. Try to do what is honorable in everyone's eyes.
  —Romans 12:17

No foul language is to come from your mouth, but only what is good for building up someone in need, so that it gives grace to those who hear.
  —Ephesians 4:29

THE CAST

Isa (aka Wolf) O'Toole—*Fifteen-year-old son of Jack O'Toole, whose quest is to venture alone into the great frontier of the North Platte River country. Isa translates to wolf in the Comanche tongue.*

Jack O'Toole—*Thirty-two-year-old son of Joseph and Kate O'Toole and father to Isa. He strives to carve a life from the Texas frontier on the easternmost reaches of the Comancheria. Earned the Comanche name Pohya Isa, Walks With Wolves.*

Mukwooru (aka, Spirit Talker)—*Thirty-two-year-old son of a Penateka Comanche chief camped within the heart of the Comancheria. The warrior name bestowed upon teen Wild Horse in recognition of his apparent connection with Taa Narumi (the Comanche Great Father), whom they confused with God.*

Blue Flower—*Young sister to Spirit Talker and daughter to Buffalo Hump, she's married to Jack. They have four young children: George, Isa, Peter, and Nadua.*

George Freeman—*A Black cowboy driving cattle north,*

and later an Army scout. He establishes a ranch on the North Platte River in Wyoming. Father to Jack and Esmeralda. Adopts the Lakota child, Zebediah.

Running Waters—*George Freeman's Pawnee wife.*

Esmeralda Freeman—*George's and Running Waters's ten-year-old daughter.*

Zebediah Freeman—*Foundling Lakota son to George and Running Waters.*

Jack Freeman—*Fifteen-year-old son of George and Running Waters.*

Kate—*Jack's seventeen-year-old sister, now married to Will Smith.*

Buck—*Jack's fourteen-year-old brother.*

Juan Perez—*Creative, hard-nosed Mexican cook on Jack's trail drive.*

Shorty McBride—*Drover on Jack's Crusade, who lives up to his nickname.*

Hardy Sullivan—*Grizzled Texas Ranger who becomes friends with Jack and finds God.*

Zeb (Zebediah)—*A wolf that Jack believes is a gift from God. They develop an ever-closer bond as the Frontier Chronicles evolve.*

Taabe—*Wolf offspring of Zebediah. Mate to Mua.*

Tathanka (aka Buffalo Man)—*Oglala Lakota warrior that captures and befriends Isa O'Toole.*

Awentia (aka Morning Star)—*Daughter of Lakota warrior Wapitiyu Okle (Spotted Elk) and granddaughter to Chief Lone Horn.*

Sergeant Blake Rawls—*Professional soldier assigned to keep an eye on Isa during the Yellowstone Expedition.*

Tatanka Wiiyaska (aka Buffalo Killer)—*Lakota warrior to whom Awentia is promised.*

Wičhóunta Elk (aka Spotted Elk)—*Miniconjou Lakota who is Morning Star's father.*

Hotamo'e (aka Bull Elk)—*A rogue Northern Cheyenne warrior.*

Historical Characters

William Tecumseh Sherman—*Famed Union general from the War Between the States, whom President Grant assigns to subdue the tribes of the Great Plains.*

Tasunke Witko (aka, Crazy Horse)—*Future chief of Oglala Lakota of the Sioux Nation. He is about 19 years old at the time of this story, but already gaining the attention of tribal leaders. He will go on to lead the massacre of General Custer's troops at Little Bighorn (aka, Greasy Grass) in 1876.*

Tatanka Iyotake (aka, Sitting Bull)—*Chief and medicine man of Hunkpapa band of Lakota Sioux.*

George Armstrong Custer—*Flamboyantly famous US Army officer and cavalry leader who performed valiantly in the War Between the States and early Indian Wars but is massacred at Little Bighorn.*

Red Cloud—*Highly regarded Chief of the Oglala Lakota nation who led the defeat of the US Army at the Fetterman Fight in 1866. His warriors also fought at Little Bighorn.*

Sitting Bull—*Hunkpapa Lakota holy man and chief who inspired the plains tribes to fight the White settlers. His warriors help defeat General Custer at Little Bighorn.*

Quanah Parker—*Chief of the Quahadi band of the Comanche nation. Son of Comanche Chief Peta Nocona and White captive Cynthia Ann Parker.*

Colonel David Stanley—*Commander of Fort Laramie in 1873 and leader of the Yellowstone Expedition to survey for the Northern Pacific Railroad.*

Isa's journey from Texas to the North Platte River country

The route used by Isa on his journey north from Texas as spawned from his vision quest. It featured challenging landscapes and many tribes known to be hostile.

THE WOLF'S QUEST: ISA'S ADVENTURE BEGINS

You Are Invited

Dear Reader,

A teen half-breed, a one-man pony, a warrior woman, and a wolf tame the 1870s frontier. That about sums up my story. If you're reading the Wolf Tales series, then it's likely that *Perilous Trails* and my pa's Frontier Chronicles series must have fully grabbed you. This first part of my tale begins in 1873, following my leaving home after a vision quest. I am fifteen years old but a grown man by frontier standards. Motivated by having had to kill a murderous Mexican *pistolero*, I left my family to embark on my own adventure of personal discovery.

The Wolf's Quest: Isa's Adventure Begins shares the testing of my courage, faith, endurance, pure grit, and search for a life mission. My folks named me Isa, which translates in Comanche to Wolf. I expect that I should add that my pa is White and my ma is a Comanche. That makes me, my twin brother George, brother Peter, and young sister Nadua what folks called half-breeds. As you'll find out, this can be a blessing and a heavy burden.

Do keep in mind that my story incorporates history not found in most school history books. This book relates my tale as driven by fate and guided by God.

I have met up with plenty of Indians, especially Comanche and Lakota Sioux, so you'll find me using some of their language throughout *The Wolf's Quest*. I have provided a handy glossary of Comanche and Lakota words toward the back of this book. I also provide a handy glossary of frontier terms.

I'm a Christian, but I have tried to grasp the Comanche and Lakota cultures to better understand them. The Indian religion is based upon what is referred to as *animism*, in which every common natural item, from fish and animals to plants, trees, waterways, and mountains, were believed to have souls or spirits. The spirits and traditions connected with them guided the Comanche and Lakota. Their passion for their spirits no doubt gave them their fearlessness, as fed by the belief that they were protected in everything they did. Would they kill to defend their beliefs? Theirs was not a religion of love and forgiveness.

Could Indians like the Comanche or Lakota become Christians? My story in *The Wolf's Quest* shares my personal evolution at the intersection of faith and culture. It was like Saint Patrick's conversion of the Irish to Christianity, folding many of their less offensive heathen rites into the Catholic faith. Would this work with the Indians? Well, it's part of the story.

As you follow my adventures, ask yourself whether you might be up to meeting the challenges I take on. Dangers? Privations? Hmmm. How might you have fared? Through it all, I first relied on the teachings from my family, then went on to learn from the raw and risky experiences I faced. I learned to trust in instincts forged from my biblical lessons.

To be straight here, I had no idea that my story was going to fill multiple volumes until I began to write it all down. I invite you to follow my adventures on America's western frontier.

Kindest regards,
   Isa *Wolf* O'Toole.

PROLOGUE

There was no enjoying the majestically beautiful mountains, rolling green hills, and lush forests. Fresh air tinged with aromas of pine, granite rocks, cliff-like escarpments, deep crevices, and bubbling creeks were now obstacles. I had invoked the name of the mighty Oglala Lakota Chief Crazy Horse, and that seemed to have intrigued Buffalo Man enough to not have me killed on the spot. My pa had told me of his tenuous friendship with Tasunke Witko, who'd subsequently grown in stature among his *numunuu* to rival Red Cloud and Sitting Bull. "Isa *wasake sunipu*," I said, mixing Lakota and Comanche, to assure them my medicine was strong.

One of Buffalo Man's warriors wanted to kill me and raised his lance menacingly.

I mustered what strength I could and gazed upon Buffalo Man. "Tasunke Witko," I invoked again. I pushed out my chest as best I could, despite the pain from a punch I'd taken to my stomach.

Buffalo Man raised his hand to stop the warrior who was insisting on killing me. There was now silence but for the fluttering tree leaves, the meandering river, and the collective breathing of six quite fearsome-looking Oglala Lakota warriors. Buffalo Man was obviously considering what to do with me. "Tasunke Witko," he said almost reverently. "Tathanka no *wiiyuka*."

I didn't know it at the time, but *wiiyuka* translated to *coward*. Buffalo Man was a proud warrior and would not strike a defenseless prisoner. I could only hope for the best. I hadn't been terribly mistreated except for a couple of punches. To his credit, I think Buffalo Man believed that hitting a defenseless prisoner was a cowardly act better left for the women to perform.

We headed west. I tripped and fell twice in the first mile or so, but was yanked roughly to my feet. I crossed and nearly tripped again on what I gathered were ruts from wagons traversing the Oregon Trail. Every now and then, a Lakota warrior would ride alongside me, make a threatening face at me, growl in the Lakota tongue, and even spit toward me. Within the depths of my soul, silent prayers to Christ were churning.

They'd prodded and pulled me along for what I judged to be about ten miles. Buffalo Man had even directed warriors to give me water twice along the way. I continued to pray. Was this a God test? His plan? Was this part of the outcome of my vision quest? Somewhere out in the rugged landscape that surrounded me, Paint and Taabe would likely—I hoped—be following me.

Buffalo Man stopped us at the crest of a hill and had me brought beside his pony. Down below us, the sun shone its late afternoon glow on nearly a hundred teepees. He pointed. "Tasunke Witko," he stated firmly. I saw women with clubs and switches lined up to greet me. This was similar to the Comanche way of treating captives. I was about to meet my fate.

Chapter 1

Trade

Buffalo Man's small but mighty band of warriors proudly escorted me into the Oglala Lakota village. They'd even refreshed their warpaint so as to make the best impression possible. Ponies pranced under the warriors with nervous anticipation. Any time I seemed to slow down, a harsh tug would quickly correct the error of my ways. Somewhere among the vast assemblage of teepees was that of Crazy Horse. Getting there, if in fact that was Buffalo Man's intention, would be a challenge.

From the expressions on the faces of the gauntlet of women ahead of me, they were fully relishing the beatings they were about to inflict.

Buffalo Man led the way, sitting proudly erect on his pony. His white face paint was punctuated with vertical red stripes. His warriors were equally proud at their hunt having bagged a captive. There were a lot of puffed chests. We entered the gauntlet. I could sense a diabolical smile on Buffalo Man's face.

The switches applied by the women stung, but they

fell just short of cutting my skin. There'd be plenty of welts. Among the first few women, at least one wielded a club. I felt that! Staggered a little, I plodded on. A tug on my tether ever-reminded me to keep moving.

"*Enákiya!*" came a shout, delivered with authority. It apparently meant *stop*, as the thrashing instantly ceased. Through swollen eyes, I made out a tall, simply attired figure. I reckoned him for a shaman of some power.

Buffalo Man exchanged a few words with the man who'd delivered the command. He animatedly motioned toward me several times. Finally, Buffalo Man dismounted and ordered me pulled over to him.

Half staggering and stumbling, I found myself in the presence of a Lakota of quietly strong stature. There was no question as to the confidence exuding from his command presence. Despite his penetrating gaze, there was a humbleness about the man.

"Isa *onaa* Pohya Isa," I managed through bloodied lips. "Lakota *pabi.*" In my best Comanche, I tried to communicate that I was the son of Walks with Wolves and a *pabi*— a friend—of the Lakota.

Plain as he appeared, the man was obviously more than a shaman. He stared intently at my face. His eyes focused in on my bear claw necklace. Finally, his eyes lit up. "Pohya Isa! *Jiji!*" he declared. He immediately ordered me to be unbound, and his command was unhesitatingly obeyed.

I shook out my arms a bit to restore circulation.

"Tasunke Witko," he said, with a finger to his breast. "*Kola!*" he added with a hug.

I reckoned that Crazy Horse recalled my pa and that *kola* translated to friend. I was of a mind that my prayers were being answered, and I was not to become a slave to the Lakota women. The chief's recognition apparently placed great value on me.

"*Kata mato?*" he asked, pointing to my necklace.

I nodded. "*Kata mato,*" I echoed, gathering that it translated to killing the bear.

Crazy Horse smiled at Buffalo Man. "*Mas'óphiye,*" he declared. He looked at me, nodded, and walked away.

I have no idea what the word *mas'óphiye* translated to, but I figured that I would eventually find out. Buffalo Man sure seemed pleased at Crazy Horse's directive. He told the women to clean me up. It was a welcome relief from being whipped in the gauntlet.

I soon found myself standing inside a teepee. I must admit that it was a bit unnerving to be stripped bare and have a bunch of women washing me and treating my wounds. They did their best to clean up my buckskins. I reckoned that my tanned deer hide and my bear skin on the travois attached to Paint were likely long gone, but no one touched my necklace. It was as though it held some power.

At some point, I was deemed presentable, though it would take a couple of days for the bruises and swellings to diminish.

Buffalo Man reappeared and escorted me to the teepee of Crazy Horse.

Hearing the warrior's approach, Crazy Horse emerged. He scanned me head to toe and smiled at my improved appearance. "*Tuktel?*" he asked with a snake-like motion of his hand to mimic traveling. He wanted to know where I had been headed.

"George Freeman," I responded, saying the name as best I could through still-swollen lips.

Crazy Horse's eyes widened. "*Sapa wicasa,*" he muttered.

I knew that *sapa* was the Lakota word for black, so I reckoned he knew of whom I spoke.

Crazy Horse turned to Buffalo Man. "George *sukawaka*," he stated, as though concocting some plan.

Something was afoot, and I had no clue what it might be. I knew that *sukawaka* translated to *horse*. Regardless, I was now hopeful that cleaning me up meant that they had no intention of killing or enslaving me.

Crazy Horse invited me to join him and Buffalo Man for a meal.

As I sat managing to eat with my still-swollen chin, I listened to the two talk animatedly in Lakota. Every now and then, I could make out a word but was unable to string enough together to figure out what they were up to. The meal soon ended, and I was escorted from Crazy Horse's teepee.

As I stepped out into the daylight, I spotted a rather regal-looking figure of a man headed our way. From the deference exhibited by Crazy Horse in shuttling me away with Buffalo Man, I reckoned the approaching man was the mighty chief Red Cloud. I took as long a look as I could so as to indelibly imprint Red Cloud's face in my memory.

Buffalo Man led me to a teepee where I'd apparently reside until they were ready to implement whatever plan they'd concocted. I must say that occupying the teepee brought back early childhood memories of visits with my folks to Spirit Talker's Penateka Comanche village. The woodsmoke, tantalizing cooking smells, and aromas of tanning hides were strikingly familiar. In my brief scan of the village, I noted that the Lakota had far fewer ponies than the Comanche. I reckoned that this was more a function of the nomadic nature of my Comanche ancestors, as juxtaposed to the more stationary lives in the mountains and brutal winters that were tough on livestock.

* * *

I sat on a bed of buffalo hides. They did little to ease the pain of the bruises the Lakota had inflicted upon my body. Far as I could tell, my soul was clear. I hadn't been given any drink that might have dulled my senses.

I had no idea how long I had been sleeping, when I felt a gentle touch and warm breath beside me. Could Taabe have found his way here? No, this was not a paw stroking my chest.

I ever-so-slowly opened one eye and peeked in the direction of whatever or whoever was beside me. Imagine my shock upon seeing a young girl, a very young, very pretty girl. My eyes were now opened wide.

She saw me awaken and locked eyes with me. She gently touched my cheek, then slowly pulled back. She pointed to herself. "Awentia," she cooed breathlessly. She pointed skyward and made a star sign. Her name meant Morning Star. Then, she pointed to me. "Isa."

I'd gathered my wits. "What do you want?" I blurted in English.

She shook her head. Morning Star apparently didn't understand English. She cocked her head and smiled. Her hand reached out to stroke me, and it was headed a bit low for my comfort.

I sat bolt upright with a groan. My entire body hurt. I looked at her. She was beautiful and—oh my—stark naked. I tossed a buffalo robe over her. I wasn't ready for this. Pa had told me a little, but I had yet to muster any interest in women. I was happy with riding the range, hunting wild game, and fishing in rushing waters.

Morning Star burst into tears. I'd hurt her feelings. She thought she'd been rejected.

I shook my head and tried to give her a comforting smile. I wasn't about to hug her.

I averted my eyes as she slipped into a buckskin dress. She touched my shoulder and gave me an apologetic look.

"Awentia go," I said with a nod toward the teepee exit.

She shook her head and produced a wooden bowl filled with poultices. She pointed to my wounds. She had apparently come to care for my cuts and bruises but gotten carried away with more passionate desires.

I nodded, indicating that it was okay to apply the poultices. "Awentia *okin*," I assured her. Ma had told me that *okin* was the Lakota word for pretty.

Morning Star smiled and began to gently daub my wounds with the poultice concoction. Upon finishing, she smiled, kissed me lightly on my forehead, and departed with a look that had invitation written all over it.

My brush with a Lakota woman now put aside, I lay back and once again fell asleep. My thoughts turned to escape. Where was Paint? Taabe?

* * *

I quickly found that I was under guard. The sentries at my teepee attended their duties in two-hour shifts. Escape was not a realistic endeavor.

Bright and early on the third day of my captivity, Tathunka threw open the flap of the teepee and motioned me to follow him. As I shielded my eyes and blinked to ward off the bright sunlight, I made out a black pony they'd readied for me. Wherever we were headed, I'd be under heavy escort, as Crazy Horse himself was leading this venture. Tathunka and the six warriors who'd helped capture me were joined by four more heavily armed and painted braves. Tathunka directed me to mount the pony and not speak.

Crazy Horse led the way out of the village.

As we passed a bevy of young women, I saw Morning Star. She saw me but averted her eyes. I reckoned I wouldn't soon be forgetting her touch as she'd applied that healing poultice.

Judging from the position of the sun in the morning sky, we were headed eastward. By putting together the direction we'd traveled a couple of days before, it finally occurred to me that they intended to trade me to George, probably in exchange for horses.

We were soon following the ruts of the Oregon Trail. I'd twice spotted Taabe and Paint far off. So far as I could tell, the Lakota hadn't seen them. I was rather surprised that they hadn't tried to find Paint, given the high value placed on horses. We intersected with the North Platte River. This told me that George's ranch was nearby. We did stop to rest a couple of times.

Thus far, the Lakota had talked a bit among themselves but had said nothing to me. Buffalo Man reminded me to keep silent.

I liked the pony I was riding. He wasn't so spirited as Paint, but he was a fine, well-proportioned stallion. If I chose to escape, he'd put up a great effort. Of course, there was no point in fleeing so long as the Lakota didn't figure to harm me. I was worth more to them alive and well. In fact, I was likely worth a lot of horses. I chuckled to myself as I reminisced on my pa's story of giving Buffalo Hump more than a dozen ponies as dowry to marry his daughter. My fond memories were jolted by a murmur among the warriors. I scanned the horizon and quickly saw what had grabbed their attention. Prairie schooners were kicking up dust a couple of miles ahead of us.

"*Kata wasichus,*" growled a warrior near me.

That translated to, *kill the White man*. It caused a shudder to run up my spine. I felt certain that the Lakota would have eagerly attacked if they had more warriors.

I realized that the dust from the wagon train was settling. It had stopped. Pa had told me that wagon trains often stopped at George's ranch to rest and replenish. The Lakota halted to assay the situation. They were decked out in serious Lakota finery with plenty of paint and feathers. In fact, they were right fierce-looking. Crazy Horse stood out, as he was quite plainly attired. There was a certain majesty in his strong, quiet bearing. He didn't need fanciful adornments to assure folks that he was in command.

Tathunka was shaking his head and quietly objecting in resistance to Crazy Horse's counsel. Finally, he nodded.

Tathunka motioned me to ride beside Crazy Horse, and we slowly rode toward George's ranch. The warriors fanned out behind us as we drew within shouting distance of the house. They rode tall with chests puffed out in a show of fearlessness.

I saw a tall, well-muscled Black man standing beside a water trough near the corral beside the barn. I reckoned it must be George. What appeared to be a rifle leaned against the trough. A couple of children played on the gallery across the front of the house. My eyes went from the children to a window where the muzzle of a rifle was pointed at my escorts.

"*Thašína* George!" called out Crazy Horse in greeting.

George squinted as though trying to recognize me. He hadn't moved as yet to pick up the rifle. "Tasunke Witko *hédake*," responded George, by way of welcome. He cast a quick look at the circled wagon train a half mile away on the south bank of the North Platte. "*Thaŋníhe na wíiya*," added George, apparently asking in the Lakota tongue what Crazy Horse was seeking.

I gathered that they knew each other. It was unsurprising that George spoke the Lakota tongue, though his fluency was impressive.

Crazy Horse broke into a grin, gave a peace sign, and dismounted. "*Wíiyokiya sunkawaka*," he stated. He was ready to trade for horses.

"*Thasíyagnak yuhá kštó?*" asked George. I think he was asking what Crazy Horse wished to trade for horses.

Crazy Horse laughed and directed me to dismount. I was presented as trade goods.

George took a long, appraising look at me. I saw his eyes give a hint of recognizing me. But for my black hair, I did resemble my pa. He laid a serious gaze on Crazy Horse. "*Thannin sunkawaka?*" There was no ceremony, as would be the case with Comanche. George got right down to business.

"*Wíiyazeka*," responded Crazy Horse, holding up ten fingers with a facial expression that said this was nonnegotiable.

Much to my surprise and the shock of the Lakota warriors, George gave an equally firm look. "*Numpa*," he stated and held up five fingers.

Holy smoke, but I realized George was negotiating. Here I was a captive of the Lakota, and he was dickering for my future.

Crazy Horse smiled. "*Anp estím*," he offered with seven fingers held up.

George looked at me as though assessing my value. I barely caught his wink. He sighed resignedly, laid a thoughtful gaze on Crazy Horse, and nodded. *"Anp estím,"* he said with seven fingers raised.

Crazy Horse stepped forward and extended his hand to seal the trade in the White man's fashion. He motioned me to go to George.

George waved a couple of his cowhands over and directed them to cull out seven horses for the Lakota. It must have been quite a picture to most any bystander, as my six foot three captive frame was hustled as part of a trade.

Crazy Horse mounted up to patiently await delivery of the ponies. I must say that he looked rather regal. It took all of half an hour until the band of Lakota were able to say their goodbyes and move out with the seven horses. All considered, the trade was handled quite graciously. You'd hardly be able to sense any animosity between George and the Lakota, though I was well aware how tensions simmered under the surface. I reckon the folks looking on from the distant wagon train must have been keeping watchful eyes on the Lakota. I reckoned they were a tad nervous.

George finally turned and faced me. "Well, Isa O'Toole, you've cost me a pretty penny." He laughed heartily and gave me a hug.

As if on signal that all was well, Taabe and Paint came into view. I whistled, and they ran to my side. It was like some storybook ending straining the bounds of believability. Incredibly, the travois still held most of what I'd packed upon it despite having been dragged through some very rough country. To say I was happy would be an understatement.

Running Waters emerged from the house and rushed

to give me a welcome hug. I could tell that she was full of questions about Pa, Ma, and my brothers and sister. "*Ana o'a hi'it?*" she asked.

I nodded. You bet I was hungry. I took a step toward the house, but paused. I looked at Paint and Taabe. They were incredibly loyal. Taabe would follow me into the house like a dog, but Paint needed extra attention.

Running Waters understood. "Keep food warm," she assured me.

George and I headed to the barn to curry Paint and unload the travois. He was overjoyed when I gifted him with the bearskin. He wrapped it around his shoulders despite the warm day. "This is special, Isa. Thank you." George looked at Taabe as he padded along with us. "You and your pa seem to have a way with wolves." As he stooped to the travois with the bearskin still draped over his broad shoulders, he drew back. "What's this?" he asked rhetorically.

I had taken the bear's head. "Thought I might make myself a hat for winter," I understated.

"That's going to make quite a chapeau, Isa," he observed.

"Chapeau?"

George laughed. "That's Frenchy talk for hat." He turned to Taabe. "How'd you come upon this fellow?"

"Taabe appeared during my vision quest. I think it's a God thing," I mused.

"You were very lucky that Tasunke Witko recalled meeting your pa. It wasn't under the best of circumstances," advised George. "The chief has been working side-by-side with Red Cloud to stir things up a might. I don't understand why they didn't take your horse."

I chuckled. "Paint is a one-man pony, Mr. Freeman. I think they knew it. Besides, they're not tied to the nomadic life like the Comanche. The Comanche would have done whatever it took to capture Paint."

George shook his head in wonderment. "I still think it's just not like the Lakota to pass on a good piece of horseflesh. Oh, and you should just call me George. Lose that Mr. Freeman greeting." He laughed. Any ice had been broken.

"With Taabe's presence, I think the leader of the hunting party wasn't sure about my *sunipu*. I also kept calling Tasunke Witko's name, and that seemed to unsettle him a bit."

"That could very well be so," George said, with a thoughtful nod. "Let's get Paint settled in and grab some grub," said George, shifting the subject. "Maybe, we can work on that bear hat. Wearing a lid like that would scare the dickens out of any Indian in his right mind. It marks you as a man not to be trifled with."

I smiled at that. I guess God would forgive a bit of pride. It's pridefulness that causes problems.

Chapter 2

Welcome

I had been instantly and warmly welcomed by the Freeman family. George and Running Waters had two children. Jack was about my age, and Esmeralda was around ten. Given that I was a blend of White and Comanche, it fascinated me to see the mix of Black and Pawnee in their children. While Jack had mostly Pawnee features but dark skin, Esmeralda took her appearance from George. Blessedly, she was quite petite, as God spared her George's broad, well-muscled shoulders and rather tall stature. As we sat, ate, and conversed, I found myself ever more comfortable.

"What of the folks from the wagon train up on the river?" I asked.

"They come visit later," advised Running Waters. "They see Lakota. Much fear."

I cogitated on how folks stopping by must be taken aback by the big smiling Black man whom they turned to for advice and resupply. "Pa told me about y'all's experiences with wagon trains years back. No telling what sorts of people might be making more ruts on the Oregon Trail."

"Rarely have any trouble. The war settled most folks, though there are a few still fighting it. By the time they reach us, they're trail-weary. Their needs triumph over any lingering animosities. With the wave of Whites that has swept in looking for gold, the tribes are riled up. Indians are a greater worry to the wagon trains."

"What about y'all and the tribes?" I queried.

"They don't bother us so much. The old agent Twiss was a help with that. Your pa, too. The Lakota are savvy enough to appreciate our beeves and horses. They trade for livestock, cookware, and guns. Your pa's friend Tasunke Witko keeps his people under control." George paused with a serious glance at Running Waters. "We have observed increasing tensions among the tribes. It seems that President Grant has ordered General Sherman to bring the Indians of the frontier under control so as to keep White settlers safe."

"Is that William Tecumseh Sherman?"

George nodded.

"He's a tough one. Pa said that his scorched-earth strategy during the War Between the States hastened the war's end." I let George know that I was somewhat informed.

"The Oglala Lakota, Northern Cheyenne, Hunkpapa Sioux, Crow, and Arapaho feel seriously threatened. I've heard of war talk among important chiefs like Red Cloud, Crazy Horse, and Sitting Bull. Sherman latched onto a Colonel Ranald MacKenzie down in Texas, who has gained a reputation as an Indian fighter of considerable repute. Add in a glory-seeking officer like George Custer, and you have a recipe for big trouble."

"So, you think there'll be war?" I asked.

George nodded, then changed the subject. "Has Jack seen to you being baptized?"

I laughed. "Pa told me about the Cheyenne attack during the baptism in the North Platte."

"Well, we'll see that doesn't happen again," he responded with a smile. He thought on the incident, then laughed. "You ready to commit to your faith?"

I nodded.

"I'll take that as a yes," replied George. "Meanwhile, we'll give you a tour of our fine spread."

"Wait," interjected Running Waters.

George and I turned to her with curious expressions.

"Isa fifteen years old. His father tell us he kill *pistolero*. He kill bear. He be man now and have man name."

I recalled my ma telling me of this Comanche custom. I sure didn't want some name like Bear Killer. "I like my name," I insisted. Isa was the Comanche word for wolf, and I was proud of it.

George looked from Running Waters to me. Jack and Esmeralda looked on with anticipation. "Running Waters speaks truth of old ways. We prepare for a new world out here with new ways. If Isa likes his name, let it be his man name."

Running Waters nodded her agreement.

"Let's take that tour," I urged.

* * *

Happy couldn't begin to describe my joy that the Lakota had not taken Paint from me. Had they truly wanted him, they could have shot and killed Taabe and then easily captured my Pinto stallion. I suspect that Buffalo Man was so taken with capturing me that he momentarily forgot about my horse. He was intent on bringing his prize to his people.

George, his son Jack, and I, saddled up and headed northward toward the wagon train. Taabe followed behind us. As we rode, I took in the crisp mountain air and the lush grasses that were the product of heavier-than-typical late summer rains. We must have presented quite a sight as we approached the wagon train. A Black cowboy, a Black/Pawnee teen, and a White/Comanche teen were undoubtedly unexpected.

A grizzled White man emerged from the circle of wagons and raised a hand.

We reined in perhaps fifty feet away.

"Welcome to the Circled Cross Ranch," announced George.

I hadn't heard the name of his spread before and rather liked it.

"Name's Ike Walton. I'm the wagon master. Got a few sick folks here, so y'all had best stay clear."

George nodded. He'd encountered this sort of situation before. Entire wagon trains might be hit with cholera or smallpox. The collateral damage that most folks didn't consider was what such diseases did to the Indians. "Y'all need anything?" Of course, he knew that they did.

Walton nodded. "We could use some flour and would be pleased to pay for two of your choice cattle."

"We'll see that you get all you need, Mr. Walton." George grew deadly serious. "Y'all are headed into very hostile territory. I suggest that y'all tighten guards at night and have good men riding point. The Lakota and Northern Cheyenne pose great danger. Y'all have a fair-sized train, so they'll think twice about attacking during the day."

"Much obliged," replied Walton.

"Y'all tend to the sick. It sure ain't fun traveling this country for folks battling sickness." George began to turn away, then paused. "Winter is coming on, Mr. Walton. If y'all reckon to make it to Oregon before the passes close up, you'd best hurry."

We turned our horses and headed toward the Circled Cross Ranch western range. George turned to me as we rode. "Those folks have a tough journey ahead. Likely, many won't make it, especially the sick. If the Indians don't get them, the sickness will." He said it matter-of-factly but drove home his point. George looked off wistfully toward the mountains. "If disease doesn't finish them, it'll surely finish the Indians." A strong breeze gusted across the pasture. Off in the distance, a longhorn bull bellowed. George looked off wistfully. "It's only September," he sighed. "Going to be a tough winter. Lost nearly a hundred head last winter. Keeping them well-fed and reasonably warm tain't easy."

"Can you protect them?" I asked.

"We built shelters a couple years back, but the beasts aren't always savvy enough to use them. Horses ain't much better."

I took in the information. George's experience confirmed what my pa had told me about avoiding the winters on the northern prairies and mountains. Freezing temperatures and deep snows endangered man and beast. Even the buffalo with their thick fur were not immune. Animals sought protection and forage in valleys shielded from the worst that Old Man Winter could dish out.

Riding the boundaries of the Circled Cross Ranch made for a long day in the saddle. George twice pointed out Northern Cheyenne hunting parties. Neither Jack nor I had spotted them.

"They're not interested in us today," noted George. He looked off at the sun, waiting to be sucked in by the western horizon. There was already a pinkish glow hanging in the sky.

We cared for the horses, cleaned up as best we could, and headed to the big house to enjoy dinner.

Running Waters greeted us at the door with an uncharacteristically serious expression. She handed what appeared to be a telegram to George.

"Say Isa, this is from your pa. He says the Fourth Cavalry attacked a big village of Quahadi and Kotsoteka Comanche on the Red River. Killed a couple dozen warriors, captured women and children, and seized horses." He hung his head sadly. "Man's inhumanity to man. They burned everything. They left the Comanche destitute. Many will starve."

I hung my head with sadness. I didn't know any Quahadi or Kotsoteka, but they were nevertheless of my *numunuu*. I could never forget that half of me was Comanche, though my soul was fully with them.

Standing there on the gallery, George looked off toward the still-lingering wagon train. "Sometimes, I wish I could turn them back."

I'd heard about how settlers in Texas fled the depredations of Comanche and Lipan Apache and how it had paralyzed the cattle industry. In the post-war chaos, military posts had not been regarrisoned quickly enough. This left ranchers and farmers terribly vulnerable. We'd seen a bit of it at Rising Cross Ranch, but were ready for any hostilities. I recalled hearing about General Sherman's stunning delivery of justice against the Kiowa bands led by Satank, Satanta, and Addo-etta last year near the Red River in Texas. The general had seen to their punishment for the gory ambush of a wagon train. Texans had finally convinced Sherman of the devastating attacks against settlers in Texas, and the general was fully committed to solving the problem using the considerable might of US troops. An attempt by Washington, DC, to bring peace to the plains by employing Quaker Indian agents had failed miserably. "It won't help, George," I said flatly. "The Indian's days are ever fewer. That General Sherman down in Texas will soon be threatening the Lakota and Cheyenne."

George nodded. "You're right, Isa." He'd known that truth deep within his heart. "The tribes are of another age. Ancient, to be sure. The industrial might of the United States will win out in the end. Such is the way of the world and probably God's plan."

* * *

My welcome to the North Platte country had certainly been far from uneventful. When I awakened from a dinner-induced sleep, the sun had just peeked above the hills to the east. I walked out onto the gallery, breathed the crisp mountain air, and looked northward. The wagon train was gone. I prayed that they'd make it through the mountains before the onset of winter. I had become addicted to coffee at home, so enjoying Running Waters's brew was second nature. As I savored her coffee and took in its aroma mixed with a fresh breeze wafting off the North Platte River, I thought further on General William Tecumseh Sherman. I prayed that the scorched-earth tactic he'd employed during the War Between the States wouldn't be applied against the *numunuu*...my *numunuu*. I couldn't yet know that it would be worse.

"Good morning and welcome to Circled Cross Ranch, Isa." Words floated behind me. It was George's daughter, Esmeralda. She was young, but would soon be of a marrying age. That was the nature of the frontier. We all grew up fast. Esmeralda would be the beautiful bride of some lucky soul. Pity any man who abused her, as George's wrath would exact justice.

"Good morning," I responded. I looked into her vibrant eyes. Beautiful. For a second, I thought back to Morning Star. My fifteen-year-old brain had begun to think of girls as more than playmates.

"Ma has breakfast ready." Her words broke my momentary hypnotic state. "I made the bear sign," she added proudly. She grabbed my elbow and pulled me inside.

I nearly tripped but saved my coffee and made it to the table. George and Jack were already seated and awaiting my arrival. In the center of the table were platters with heaps of eggs, biscuits, venison sausage, and the all-important bear sign. Running Waters refilled my coffee.

With everyone seated, George blessed the meal, and we dug in.

We made small talk. It was a process of getting more intimately acquainted. I reckoned to spend the winter here, so I would need to make myself useful. I sensed that my vision quest was far from over, and the visit here at Circled Fross Ranch was but a port of call in my journey. Being the son of George's friend didn't excuse me from carrying my weight with chores. As thoughts of helping with ranch tasks floated through my mind, George stood.

"Got a few things to handle in the barn," he announced. He looked at Jack and me.

"Er...can I help?" I offered.

George grabbed his hat and headed out the door. We dutifully followed. Once in the barn, George handed us shovels. I'd done this mucking task before, so I didn't need to be told. I entered a stall, pushed a horse's hind quarters away, and went to work.

"Pleased to have you young men together," noted George.

I must say that I appreciated being referred to as a young man, but I had the feeling that George had some serious talking in mind.

"I'm pleased that you arrived here when you did, Isa. It gives me a better excuse for handing out life advice." He delivered the last sentence with a broad, tooth-filled smile that my pa talked about.

My pa had filled the heads of me and my brothers with all sorts of life advice, but I eagerly awaited what George had to say. I heard him grunt as he pushed a stack of hay into the barn. It was wrapped so as to be what might loosely be called a bale.

"*Carpe diem*," he announced. "That means seize the day. Every day, God presents us with new opportunities. We have a choice as to whether to seize them, but we must first be able to recognize them."

Well, that sure made sense. I paused and leaned on my shovel. I had an urge to say *so what* but wisely kept my mouth shut.

"We must ask ourselves whether the opportunity stirs our passions and inspires passions for some greater good. Then and only then can we decide our course of action. We alone must decide whether we have the strength to take us where the opportunity leads. Why strength? Opportunity can be surrounded with uncertainty and make us uncomfortable. Our choice demands discernment, the ability to make sound judgment."

I strove to digest George's words. He was right, of course. It got me to thinking on my vision quest. Where was it taking me? Would there be a sign to move on? Would I recognize it?

"We owe it to God to seek the best in what He's offered us. We must recognize what's true, what works, and what is possible. We must hang onto hope, for a man without hope is lost. And truth. The truth will set you free."

"Many people give up. Why?" I asked.

There was that broad smile again. George shook his head knowingly.

Jack smiled. He knew what was coming.

"Many times, folks get lured to fake happiness like moths to lanterns. They get hung up on attaining pleasures, possessions, being popular, achieving prestige, and amassing the trappings of power. Whether they achieve all that or not, they are invariably dismayed at how hollow it all is. To not achieve their view of happiness leads to despair and loss of hope. To achieve it? Same outcome." George paused.

We'd stopped mucking and were hanging on his words.

"What are they missing?" I asked.

"Purpose. A mission," advised George. "Your pa found it, Isa. He was determined to fight against slavery, to fight racial prejudice in general, whether against Indians, Blacks, or Hispanics. It gave him great satisfaction even though his reach was limited. You can bet he's still pursuing that mission." George laid a steady gaze upon me. "He instilled it in you and your brothers. I'm only reinforcing it here. Both you young men will find a purpose that will drive your lives. That purpose will bring you great satisfaction, and in that is true happiness. Remember Christ noting that the path to the truth is narrow. The path to unhappiness, to false joy, is broad and fraught with all manner of evil temptations. They can be hard to resist. Your faith will be tested. Opportunity will come to you. Will you be able to seize it? *Carpe diem.*"

"*Carpe diem,*" I echoed. Doggone, but my pa and George are brilliant men.

George wasn't quite finished. "And when you do find it, you'll be faced with how to use it. Will you be called upon to influence others, and how might you do that? Never forget that you have the ability to change the world simply by what you say. All this you both will learn in due time. Always try to look through God's eyes." He threw a pitchfork full of straw into a stall. "We'll head up to the river later and do a bit of baptizing. Let's finish up here and grab some coffee before we head out."

CHAPTER 3

COLD WATERS

George, Jack, and I neatly folded our clothes and stacked them on the south bank of the North Platte River. Our weapons were laid carefully atop our clothes. George went into the frigid, rushing waters ahead of us. Jack and I would take turns. We were wary of any repeat of what happened many years back, when my pa and Spirit Talker were baptized in this very same place. In the midst of Spirit Talker being plunged under the waters, a Northern Cheyenne warrior emerged from the forest and charged toward them with decidedly hostile intent. But for my pa's quick action, one or more of the three might have been killed.

Taabe sat alongside the stacks of clothes. His blue eyes scanned the horizon while his uplifted nose sniffed for danger. No Northern Cheyenne would be interrupting this baptism.

I plunged into the waters. Dang, but they were icy cold. George baptized me in the name of the Father, Son, and Holy Spirit. Admittedly, I was anxious to get clear of the cold waters to take in the warmth of the sunbaked riverbank, so I dashed from George's grasp as quickly as I could. Jack followed, and we were soon lying back on solid land and drying out. I appreciated the meaning of baptism as my commitment to my faith, but my body didn't especially appreciate the dramatic temperature shift.

"It's downright beautiful here," I observed as I scanned the rolling prairies and surrounding mountains.

George smiled, as was his habit. I think he'd smile in the midst of battling Indians. "There's a place northwest of here that's incredibly different. I think it's where God experimented on what his creation was going to look like. Folks call it the Yellowstone."

"Can we go?" I asked.

"Have to wait until spring, Isa. It's a long trek to Yellowstone. It's better than two weeks each way, and you'd want time to explore the country. We'd be returning in the midst of winter's fury."

"Fury?" I asked.

George and Jack laughed. "Your pa never experienced our winter. He'd drive cattle up here and head home before winter," responded George.

"It's that rough?" I persisted.

"We get drifts of snow higher than your head," added Jack.

"And cold enough to freeze your words in midair," George added with a chuckle. "Cows have been known to give milkshakes." George laughed harder.

"I think I understand. Still, I really want to see the country up here."

"Let's get dressed, and we'll talk more about it."

We began the long walk back to the house with Taabe leading the way. Off to the east, we could see another wagon train coming up the Oregon Trail. With any luck, they'd make it through the passes before the winter snows made them impassable. It seemed to me that a lot of living in this country revolved around the weather.

"Trouble's brewing, Isa. The powers in Washington have decided that the Indian tribes are an obstacle to civilizing the frontier. I'm afraid it's going to get ugly."

"I know bands of my *numunuu* still fight in Texas. Quahadi and Kotsoteka Comanche fight, but most others have surrendered to reservation life. So it was with my uncle Spirit Talker and the Penateka."

"President Grant is intent on the tribes adapting to the ways of folks back east or be annihilated," observed George.

"Annihilated?"

"Destroyed. The Lakota and Cheyenne will put up a good fight. They recall how General George Custer and his Seventh Cavalry massacred Chief Black Kettle's Cheyenne at the Battle of Washita River, hardly more than three years ago, a way west of where we walk. About a hundred Cheyenne men, women, and children were killed and half that number taken prisoner. Black Kettle had made peace, so he never expected an attack, while Custer sought to make a name for himself. General Philip Sheridan went on to attack the last remnant of Northern Cheyenne dog soldiers and remove survivors to reservations." George expended on the government reaction to tribal predations and ensuring the safe passage of the waves of settlers heading west.

"Soldiers killed women and children," I stated flatly.

"Your friend Tasunke Witko has a nasty side himself. Only a half dozen years ago, he led Lakota and Cheyenne warriors in wiping out eighty US Cavalry and infantry under the command of Captain William Fetterman at Peno Head Ridge near Fort Phil Kearny. They called it the Fetterman Massacre. Crazy Horse has earned himself a role as a war leader of the Oglala Lakota. Trust me, he will cause big trouble in the future."

I shook my head. The dynamic was overwhelming. While simple on its surface, complexities ran deep. The incessant waves of settlers, accompanying diseases, loss of tribal lands and customs, broken treaties, and politics combined in a deadly mix that spelled doom for the Red man. "It's so sad. Pa told us that everyone who sins breaks the law. In fact, sin itself is lawlessness. He pointed it out to us in the Bible."

George smiled knowingly. "Must have been the Bible I gave him." He paused. "Paul wrote that the sins of man are obvious: sexual immorality, impurity and debauchery; idolatry and witchcraft; hatred, discord, jealousy, fits of rage, selfish ambition, dissensions, factions and envy; drunkenness, orgies, and the like. We see these things in the conflict between the Indians and Whites. Paul goes on to tell the Galatians that the fruit of the Spirit is love, joy, peace, forbearance, kindness, goodness, faithfulness, gentleness, and self-control. Against such things there is no law."

"Seems to be plenty of sin and not enough of those fruits of the Spirit," I observed.

"Treaties and more treaties. Promises kept and invariably broken. All goes well until somebody wants more. Covetousness yields to lawlessness. The ends justify the means as a point of diminishing returns is eventually reached and violence often erupts." George looked at me as though fearing that I wasn't grasping what he was saying. But my fifteen-year-old brain had absorbed most of my pa's and pa's teachings, and George's words weren't lost on me.

"So, folks are content until they want more of what

their neighbor has. Boundaries are disrespected, and lawlessness is the consequence," I mused as we neared the house.

George unleashed that big smile of his. "You're going to be a great one, Isa. I feel it in my bones. You'll find your life purpose, possibly in this vision quest you're following."

I stopped suddenly.

George and Jack took a couple of steps before halting and turning back toward me.

"Life purpose?" I asked.

George shook his head as young Jack looked at him quizzically. "Likely to be something greater than yourself done for the good of mankind. It'll be God's work, Isa. Your pa found a purpose in fighting prejudice, especially as manifest in slavery."

"I think I understand. When does this happen?" I naively asked.

"Don't know," replied George with that big smile.

"Y'all going to eat or just stand around?" came Running Waters's call from the house.

We didn't have to be asked twice. I glanced to my left and saw the wagon train continuing on its Oregon Trail journey. They just might make it through the mountains before winter sets in. I shrugged and followed George and Jack into the house. Between baptism and philosophizing, I was famished.

Chapter 4

Exploration

The countryside around the Circled Cross Ranch was incredibly clothed in its raw beauty. I yearned to explore despite the dangers that lurked. I didn't feature the idea of encountering Crazy Horse or any of the Cheyenne hunting or raiding among the mountains and forests. Still, the hills beckoned. September and October were great times to hunt back in Texas, but the terrain here around the North Platte called to me. I caught Running Waters staring at me.

"Isa itch for hills," she observed.

George nodded and looked my way. "I expect he's going to scratch it."

I shrugged. "I'll be careful." After all, what could become of a six-foot-three-inch, well-muscled teenager who'd already dealt with *pistoleros*, battled a grizzly, and came out relatively unscathed against warlike Oglala Dakota? In deep thought, I absentmindedly stroked my bear claw necklace.

"Just remember that you're not immortal, Isa," Counseled George. I think he was feeling an obligation to protect the son of his friend. I caught his signal to Jack.

"Maybe, I could go," suggested George's young son.

This development created an awkward situation for me. I really wanted to explore by myself. While Jack was my age, I felt that he wasn't quite so grown up as me. Perhaps, I had simply matured faster by virtue of the adventures already packed into my young life. I'd killed that *pistolero* in battle, fought and killed the bear, and endured capture by hostile Lakota. My brain spun as I sought a reason to refuse his companionship. My eyes flitted searchingly from George to Running Waters to Jack to Esmeralda. The uncomfortable pause in conversation seemed like hours, even though it was mere seconds. "Thanks kindly, Jack, but I expect y'all recall that I'm following my vision quest. I really need to be exploring by myself as I find my way." I felt bad afterward, as Jack looked just a tad hurt.

George sighed. "Not to worry, son. We'll go hunting while Isa here is roaming the hills." He turned to me. "I'll sketch you a map with key landmarks, Isa. You likely share your pa's sense of direction, but it'll help guide you."

All was settled. "I reckon I'll head out in the morning. Likely spend a couple of days traipsing around. I'll go wherever God points me," I said with a warm but determined smile.

We finished up dinner with warm apple pie. I was feeling right at home with the Freeman family. I was grateful that we managed to get beyond uncomfortable situations like we'd just experienced, as we'd be spending a long, snowy winter together.

* * *

Shards of sunlight pierced the folds of drapery hanging from the window above my head. I'd been blessed with a solid night of sleep. I figured it was partly due to that warm apple pie. We'd bedded down early despite spending a coupler of hours after dinner gathered around the hearth, as George led a discussion of whether it was moral for men seeking gold to violate the treaties with the Indians. It was thought-provoking. Of course, we considered it in the context of what Jesus might have done. We pretty much knew his inclinations but could only guess. George made the case that the tribes were not a sovereign nation with land boundaries and a central government. President Grant determined that it was illegal to squat on reservation lands, however, the Indians didn't own the land, and that made the treaties invalid. It made for an intellectual kerfuffle.

These thoughts swirled in my brain as my eyes adjusted to the light. I swung my feet to the floor and reached for my boots. I slipped on the left boot, then paused. Taabe had his ears erect and was giving me a strange look. I shrugged and shook out the right boot. A scorpion fell to the floor and scurried away. Taabe relaxed. I would have stomped the critter, but it was early and I wasn't quick enough. Avoiding a nasty sting would have to serve as satisfaction enough.

After a hearty breakfast, I headed to the barn to saddle Paint. I had prepared my supplies and double-checked my possibles bag. Running Waters gave me a sack loaded with jerky and pemmican to satisfy my appetite on the trail. She even tossed in a couple of those delectable bear sign treats. The .56 caliber Spencer carbine was loaded and nestled in its scabbard off my saddle horn. My trusty Colt Peacemaker that Pa had given me just about the time I headed out on my vision quest was comfortably holstered on my hip. I decided to bring my bow and quiver of arrows, as I appreciated the silence such a weapon afforded for hunting or defense. My weaponry was completed with the Bowie knife sheathed at my back. The weather still figured to be temperate, so I eschewed both vest and jacket. The nights would be cool, but a blanket would suffice to keep me plenty warm. With the uncertainties concerning possible hostile Indians, it would make sense for me to mostly cold camp.

I led Paint to the gallery where George and the rest of the Freemans stood to bid me farewell on my brief adventure into the Laramie Mountains to the west of George's ranch. They gave hugs all around, with George waiting to be last. "Go with God, Isa," he counseled, and looped a leather lanyard over my head with a carved cross hanging from its front. It fell neatly among the bear claws. "Keep an eye out for Cheyenne war parties. The dog soldiers are no more, but there are remnants. If you're not wary, they'll likely see you before you see them. They'd as soon kill you as look at you."

His advice would have scared most men, but I was young, felt immortal, and had faith that God would protect me. God's protection was likely so, but He surely looked for my assisting Him by being alert to danger. "Thank you, George. See y'all in a few days." I climbed up into Paint's saddle. Taabe gave a *woof* as though impatient to be on the trail. I turned Paint's head westward, and we rode off. I turned a couple of times to see the Freeman family still standing on the gallery watching my departure.

* * *

It took the better part of the day to reach the foot of the mountain range. I had followed the Oregon Trail, noting the ruts etched into rocks at various places along the route. Here and there were broken wagon wheels, pieces of abandoned furniture, and sadly, graves. I looked to the forests around me. I recalled my pa telling me how the soldiers building Fort Laramie used to haul wood from near here for construction. They'd chop down trees near the base of the Laramie Mountains and haul the logs to the fort. The day's journey placed them at the mercy of the Indians. I scanned the surrounding area. There were plenty of places among the deep ravines and thick stands of aspen and spruce for Indians to set their ambushes. I reckoned wood detail was like a death sentence, yet they did complete the fort. It had stood off and on as a guardian to the Oregon Trail since its beginnings as a trading fort back in 1834. My pa had told us that it was frequented by famous mountain men like Jim Bridger back when the mountains were home to hearty men trapping beaver.

I looked up at the rocks and stands of spruce that stared down at me from their lofty perches. A couple of big horn sheep leaped among the rocky outcroppings. Behind me on the rolling prairie grazed a herd of perhaps five hundred or more buffalo. I decided that this would be a great spot to camp. The mountains could wait until morning. Taabe sniffed around the perimeter as if to ensure that the location was safe. "We'll cold camp," I assured him. It didn't take long around this country to find yourself in hostile territory.

A buck ventured within shooting distance of my arrows. Doggone critter must have reckoned he was safe, as I wasn't making a cooking fire. I'd enjoy a dinner of jerky and pemmican.

With Taabe ever on alert, I managed to catch some much-needed sleep.

* * *

The day broke in its full glory. There's little else to stoke the appreciation of God's wonders than a breeze running through the leaves of a stand of quaking aspen, as contrasted to a backdrop of huge jagged boulders. Yes, it would be a great day for heading up into the Laramie Range. The change from the grassy rolling hills had been rather sudden. The grass was greener, and there were still wildflowers. Peering out from under the brim of my hat, I saw no sign made from human presence. The steep slope served to ensure my great care as to awareness of my surroundings. I hoped I might find some hidden cave-like spot where I could build a fire and bag the next overconfident buck that wandered nearby. To that end, I nudged Paint through the trees until I found a game trail, a path frequented by deer and other low-lying critters.

My vision quest had already taken life-altering turns. What might be the event that would set me on a mission, a journey of purpose? What might that be?

I expect we'd covered about ten miles. It was slow going and a test of the skill and endurance of me and my four-legged companions. We finally found a place to camp beside a rocky outcropping. It offered a clear view of the surroundings. There'd be no Cheyenne or Lakota sneaking up on me. Of course, they could overwhelm me with sheer numbers, if they were of a mind to. I counted on me not being worth their effort. For the moment, I kicked back with Taabe and looked out over an incredible vista. The hill country in my beloved Texas was beautiful, but this qualified as majestic.

Way off, I spotted a procession of prairie schooners lumbering along the Oregon Trail. Not far away from the wagon train, a band of Indians followed. I couldn't make out the tribe, but there were plenty enough hostiles to make trouble for the settlers. There was nothing I could do but watch the likely calamity unfold on the theater that was life...and death. I had a front row seat to an all-too-frequent chapter in the frontier saga. I prayed that the folks in the wagon train would survive. Perhaps the Indians would decide it wasn't a worthy target for attack. With winter but a couple of months off, the tribes would be thinking of storing meat. Buffalo and the White man's cattle were on their menu. The Comanche in me calculated that the settlers weren't an inviting enough target to lose warriors over.

I watched as the wagon train formed up into a defensive circle in preparation for camping for the night. Cattle were herded inside the circles, and cooking fires were soon pouring smoke into the air. The settlers were clueless as to the lurking threat. I observed the Indians counseling among themselves before riding off. The wagon train had been spared. I wondered whether they'd been those feared remnants of the feared Cheyenne dog soldiers. They were comprised of warriors who hated the Whites for their encroachment onto Indian lands. Even the dog soldiers weren't stupid enough to take on a prey that would inflict too much damage to their forces. With disease and the efforts of US soldiers, the warrior ranks were increasingly difficult to replenish. Were it not for the buffalo, the tribes would have already succumbed to the White onslaught.

Some thoughts were beginning to brew in my mind. My pa had initially fought to protect the Comanche from White prejudice before turning his efforts toward opposing slavery. Was I to be involved with the tribes of the northern plains? I needed to bring my thinking into greater focus. I figured to explore for another day or so before returning to the Circled Cross Ranch.

Thinking on Pa's dealings with the Comanche got me to wondering how my folks were getting on. I especially thought on my twin brother George and on Peter. Nadua was barely eleven years old and would be under Ma's watchful eyes. Pa and Ma had told me what to expect from Whites as to half-breed men, but I was clueless as to how women might be treated. It distressed me that *tosa* women held no respect for Indian women. I don't know that I'd ever quite be up to understanding that. How could supposedly Christian women be so...so un-Christian? Perhaps, the irony was that among the tribes of the frontier, my Comanche ancestors were well-known for intermarrying with other races. A Comanche might be a mix of every race to be found on the prairies. It was a consequence of the nature of their nomadic life and trading practices, as captives and slaves of other races intermarried within the tribal fabric. My uncle Spirit Talker had told me of some Comanche chiefs having several wives. They would have what might be called a primary wife and then a pecking order of other wives, often with specialized roles within the family. It surely wasn't like what my pa and ma practiced, nor here with George and Running Waters.

* * *

I didn't see any more Indians as I climbed about and strove to familiarize myself with the slopes of the Laramie Mountains. The experience had the effect of working up my considerable enthusiasm for this Yellowstone place that George mentioned. Spring couldn't come fast enough at the thought of seeing the natural wonders George had described.

I expect I'd been traveling for roughly six days by my count. I'd scratched a small notch in a stick at sunset of each day so as to keep track. I reckoned it was time to head back to George's ranch. I decided to follow the Oregon Trail eastward. No telling whom I might encounter. Maybe I'd meet another wagon train.

* * *

I was a half-day from the ranch, when I saw the point rider from a wagon train headed my way.

As we approached each other, I saw him pull a carbine from his saddle sheath. I supposed he was taking no chances. Admittedly, my buckskins and long dark hair, combined with bow and arrows and moccasins, contributed to an Indian aura about me. It never occurred to me that he might be one of those Whites for whom the only good Indian was a dead one.

My first hint was his aiming the rifle at me.

The point rider was on horseback, and his horse must have sensed Taabe, as the animal jostled his rider just as the man squeezed the trigger. A bullet buzzed over my head. The explosion from his carbine echoed among the hills. I dug my spurs into Paint and sprinted for a stand of aspen.

Another slug whizzed past me and splintered a piece of bark from the tree I'd just ridden behind. "Hey, stop shooting!" I hollered.

"Git lost Injun!" came the angry reply.

"I come in peace," I shouted back.

"Ain't no peaceful Injuns!" he yelled. "Run back to yer

Redbellies, yuh savage!" He aimed in my general direction and fired again. I smirked that he wasn't much of a marksman. I likely could have shot him with an arrow even from the distance between us.

There appeared to be no way of persuading the point rider that he was in no danger from me. I nudged Paint deeper among the trees. Taabe gave a low growl and followed us. Blessedly, the man didn't seem inclined to pursue us or to shoot again.

I saw a man ride up from behind him. There was some sort of angry exchange. If the man from the wagon train had any sense, he'd be scolding the point man not to be shooting at lone Indians, as such action could bring an entire tribe down on the wagon train. The conversation ended with the point rider sheathing the rifle and pushing on with a few suspicious side glances up at where I'd disappeared among the trees. Shame on me for wishing that those Cheyenne dog soldiers would arrive and teach him a lesson. I silently asked God to forgive the thought. I must be above such vengeful thinking, even if it seemed justifiable in a perverse sort of way.

I circled well north of the Oregon Trail. Having crossed the North Platte and followed it southeastward, I recrossed it when I'd reached a point I reckoned to be due north of George's spread. I had stayed well clear of the wagon train.

CHAPTER 5

DOG SOLDIERS?

Dark clouds were welling up behind me as I closed the distance from the river to George's house. Admittedly, it was a relief to have ventured out and returned unscathed. I urged Paint to a canter. I'd have galloped but didn't want to seem overanxious.

George and Jack were just emerging from the barn. "Lookee here, Isa made it back in one piece," chided George, nudging his young son with his elbow.

I was feeling pretty doggone good as I drew close. I grew perplexed as I saw George's eyes suddenly grow wide.

"Run for the house!" he shouted.

I slammed my heels into Paint's sides. We quickly reached full gallop. Paint nearly tossed me over his head as he planted in front of George's house. I dismounted, grabbed my Spencer, and followed George through the door. An arrow struck the doorjamb beside my head. Taabe squeezed in behind me just as the door was closed. I adjusted my eyes to the dim interior.

George was blazing angry. He poked his Spencer through a porthole and brought down one and then a second Cheyenne warrior.

I'd never seen him so enraged. I looked around. Running Waters was reloading another rifle. Tears ran down her cheeks. Where was Jack?

I turned to the window and looked out at the attacking hostiles. I was horrified to see one kneeling over Jack. The Cheyenne savage grasped the teen's hair and was about to take his scalp. I chambered a round, aimed, and put a slug in the savage's chest. The hostile loosed his grasp, but it was then that I saw the four arrows embedded in young Jack's chest.

George was like a madman as he fired round after round. Even Running Waters had stepped to a window and was pouring lead into the attackers.

By now, at least six Cheyenne had met their death. This was a very heavy toll, as there couldn't have been more than twenty to begin with. I watched a large warrior mounted on a painted pinto motion the remaining savages to back off from the attack. The apparent leader led them off a distance, then had the audacity to return alone, making a sign for peace. He wanted to collect his dead warriors. He was a fearsome sight with his face painted white with black stripes and a long leather rope trailing from one arm. I reckoned that he fancied himself a dog soldier, even though they'd been nearly wiped out about six years ago.

I watched from the window as George stepped out onto the gallery. He allowed the Cheyenne to come a little closer, then raised his rifle, aimed, and put a bullet between the savage's eyes.

I was aghast at what George had done despite understanding the reason.

The remaining Cheyenne were shocked as they pranced about on their ponies while trying to decide what to do. Some wanted to renew the attack, while others quite clearly urged full retreat. Seven Cheyenne families would be grieving this evening, and it made no sense to them to increase the tribe's suffering.

Meanwhile, George had dropped his rifle and run to his son's body. He let out a great, low wail at the Cheyenne attackers as he held the boy's head in his arms.

The hostiles finally decided they'd done enough damage. Despite their heavy losses and inability to collect the bodies of their dead, they made a bitter show of lance waving and war whoops before galloping away.

George was inconsolable. Running Waters kneeled beside him, wailing some sort of Pawnee death chant. A misty rain began to fall with dark clouds presaging heavier rains to come.

I found myself fully dismayed at the scene before me. Why had the Cheyenne attacked after so many years of living at peace with the Freemans? What could they possibly have hoped to achieve and at such terrible cost? I saw Esmeralda weeping by herself just inside the front door. I figured that I couldn't help George and Running Waters, so I eased over to console her.

My triumphant return had turned into a nightmare.

As I held Esmeralda, I watched as George gently worked each of the arrows from his son's body. A reverence hung in the air. As he removed each arrow, he kissed Jack's forehead and stroked his hair as if to soothe him from any pain.

Running Waters continued to wail, but more softly now. I feared that she might follow the custom of cutting her forearms as a further manifestation of grief, but she didn't seem so inclined.

Esmeralda's crying had turned to whimpering, as she nestled in my arms.

Within the depths of my soul, I cursed the Cheyenne. I'd killed at least two and wounded two others, but I found that their deaths did nothing to compensate for the grief hovering over us here and now. Why couldn't mankind get along peacefully? It was a question for the ages and not likely to be resolved any time soon. I let loose the tears I'd been holding back.

* * *

Three days after the attack, the Circled Cross Ranch seemed to have returned to normalcy. Young Jack had been buried on a knoll overlooking the house and the grandeur of the countryside. It was clear that George's faith remained as strong as ever. He'd surely seen much in his forty-odd years, from slavery to droving cattle to ranching. He'd buried plenty of men and women, though never figured to be burying his own son. Despite his faith, I could see that he was bleeding inside. There were no words that sufficed to bring comfort.

I observed him and Running Waters each morning as they kneeled in prayer at their son's grave.

I prayed to God for them to find solace. I was concerned for Esmeralda. She desperately needed her parents as she dealt with the loss of her brother. There was a deadness creeping into her eyes as though having given up hope.

Finally, after dinner on the fourth day following the attack, George motioned us over to the hearth.

"We are burdened with heavy hearts," he began. "Jack's death brings great sadness. His life was cut far too short. Yet, God would have us live on, to ease the yoke of our grief. We can't bring our son back, nor can we wreak vengeance on those who took his life. We must find forgiveness. Christ tells us to judge not, and you will not be judged; condemn not, and you will not be condemned; forgive, and you will be forgiven. It's not easy. Our path is the narrow one."

"Amen," I murmured reflexively.

George smiled at me, then turned to Esmeralda. "Running Waters is past child-bearing time. You, our beautiful daughter, remain as the joining of our love. We ask the Lord to give you peace, Esmeralda, for you are much loved." With that, he wrapped his big arms around her and held her tightly. "May God ever protect you and bless you with great bounty, daughter."

I found myself deeply touched by George's heartfelt expression of love.

* * *

The rains of late September were merely God's taunting us as to what was to come. Snow flurries had begun the second week of October as the weather took a decidedly chilly turn.

One last wagon train ventured through as September came to a close. George doubted they'd make it through the mountain passes before the snows set in. As many folks feared over the years, no one wished to see a repeat of the infamous Donner Party back in 1846. The Donner train found itself snowbound in the Sierra Nevada and wound up resorting to cannibalism to survive. Of eighty-seven members, only forty-eight survived. Tackling the Oregon Trail up in the high Sierras was definitely not a good decision.

We had worked doubly hard to store plenty of firewood. An important addition George had added was a shelter for the cattle. It looked more like a large baffle several feet high that was aimed at blocking wind and blizzard snows. George called it a storm baffle and had it stocked with plenty of hay. Another addition was rope lines from the bunkhouse to the big house and from the bunkhouse to the barn. The purpose was to enable George and his ranch hands to traverse the spaces among the buildings in the event of a blinding snowstorm.

I occasionally thought on the failed attack by the Cheyenne. While a handful of them may have been dog soldier throwbacks, the hatred for the Whites still lurked in their heads. I suspected that the Cheyenne, along with the mighty Lakota, would be serious trouble for settlers sooner than later.

As the days rolled on, we spent more time indoors, sheltered from frigid temperatures. A mat of snow settled over the landscape for the coming winter. George and I managed to fashion my bear's head into a downright fearsome-looking hat. Flaps flipped down over my ears, and the snout and fangs at the front were scary-looking. What I loved the most were the eyes. We'd found some obsidian and inserted the volcanic glass into the eye sockets to present a frightening gaze that bore into the very soul of anyone looking head-on at the hat. I liked it, and George seemed pleased as well. Running Waters and Esmeralda couldn't look at it.

Esmeralda? She was maturing. Women tended to mature far more quickly on the frontier than back east. It was a matter of survival. She was now eleven years old, and to her mother's chagrin, occasionally cast fanciful eyes at me.

Me? I found my thoughts drifting back to the Morning Star. Images of the beautiful Oglala Lakota girl whom I had spurned months ago, when a captive in her village, took root in my dreams. I wondered whether I'd see her again. Could it be possible that she thought about me? I doubted it, but not in the fantasies of my nights warming near the hearth in the coziness of the bunkhouse.

Did I say bunkhouse? I had decided to live as one of George's ranch hands. The food was not quite so fancy, but the company was great in that it offered me new perspectives on frontier life. Running Waters added to our humble menu, and George often joined us for meals and repartee. It's amazing how decidedly normal events can become exciting life adventures when repeated frequently enough. For example, a friendly encounter with a Kiowa warrior could escalate into a life-and-death situation with enough telling. Occasional sips of whiskey by the storyteller often added to the wildness of the stories. Rest assured, I did not imbibe.

Thus, the first months of autumn passed. The stands of aspens dotting the hills were glorious with their color, and crisp, cloudless skies greeted us most days. This having been said, I did find myself longing for Texas.

* * *

Christmas was drawing near, when I got my first taste of winter in the Rocky Mountains. We'd seen ever-more menacing clouds gathering. George gave me a knowing smile as I headed for the bunkhouse this night. He nodded at the gathering storm and told me to answer nature's call before bedding down as if to warn me that a trip to the privy might get dicey later. It was after midnight when a howling wind shook the very rafters of the bunkhouse. I heard ice pelting the sides of what I hoped and prayed was a sturdy enough structure to withstand this sort of beating. The North Platte had already begun to freeze over. In the dead of night, I could only begin to imagine what a heavy layer of snow might look like. I'd been out with the ranch hands looking for stray beeves earlier that day and seen all manner of critters use the ice as a bridge across the river. I suppose it was right convenient for them.

The steady staccato of snow and ice beating against the bunkhouse combined with Taabe's warm body stretched alongside, eventually lulled me back to sleep.

If Hap and Dred shaking me hadn't awakened me come morning, the aroma of fresh coffee would. I shook the cobwebs from my head and swung my legs from the bunk. Driven by that smell of coffee and now the sizzle of bacon, I pulled up my pants, shook out my boots by force of habit in case of critters, slipped them on, and headed for the coffee pot.

"Whoa, Isa," cautioned Dred. "Yer gonna…"

Too late! I let go of the coffee pot handle, but not before experiencing the wrath of its heat.

Dred waved a thick cloth pad at me. "Yuh should know better, son. Always use this fer the bunkhouse pot." He slathered a bit of salve on my reddened fingers, and poured coffee into a cup for me. "Now, set yoself while I whip us up some eggs to go with thet thar bacon."

"Thanks, Dred." I sheepishly eased over to a bench beside a beat-up but serviceable table and examined the bright red palm of my hand. The hand would heal quickly enough, but that table would always carry the scars of much use by cow hands and whoever owned it back when.

The bunkhouse door swung open, and a heavily wrapped Esmeralda stepped in, accompanied by a blast of snow. She slammed and latched the door behind her. "Brought y'all a treat," she announced. Running Waters had gifted we three hungry men a half dozen bear sign. The sweet treats were warmly received.

"Care fer some eggs an' bacon, young lady?" offered Dred.

"We already ate," she assured him. Esmeralda turned to me. "Father wants to see you, when you're finished with breakfast." She punctuated the message with a smile that some folks might have thought of as flirtatious. I felt sure that sort of intent was not in her nature, at least, not yet. "You boys stay warm," she said as she opened the door to face the icy journey back to the house. The wind-driven snow was near blinding. This is where those rope lines became important. She disappeared into the maw of the blizzard.

I sat scooping up delectable morsels of eggs and bacon. "Where'd you find eggs, Dred?" I asked.

"We done built a hencoop right off the side of the bunkhouse," he replied with a laugh. "Nuthin' like fresh eggs all winter long. Did the same fer the big house." He finished with a broad, near-toothless grin, "Now an' agin we nab us a fox. Lean but decent eatin'." He pointed to a row of a dozen red fox tails hanging on the wall behind the stove. "Dumb little critters try to get at our chickens."

I shoved some bear sign into my mouth and began to prepare for battling the blizzard by hauling my body along the rope on the short but freezing distance to the house to meet with George. I donned my buffalo coat and crowned my outerwear with the bear hat. With the buffalo coat and bear hat, I might have been mistaken for a bear, though a tad smaller than a grown grizzly. Those beasts could reach better than nine feet tall.

"Go get'um, Isa," called Hap as I forced my way out the door and into the full might of the blizzard. Taabe peered out from behind me, but backed away before finally following me. He was close enough that his nose seemed nearly attached to my hindquarters.

I pulled myself hand-over-hand only to find that I'd picked up the wrong rope and wound up facing the door to the barn. With a great sigh and breath that would have frozen in midair had it not been for the driving wind, I turned back. I found the proper rope and made my way to the house. I entered as quickly as I could so as to minimize the blast of winter following me into the house. Taabe dashed in behind me and made a great show of shaking the snow from his fur. Everybody took cover as ice crystals flew.

"Howdy, y'all," I exclaimed as I shook off most of the layer of snow clinging to my coat and hat. "Bit of a chill out there," I understated.

George was nursing a cup of coffee alongside the hearth, which featured a goodly fire aimed at keeping the place toasty warm. "About time you showed up," he chided. "Pull up a seat."

Esmeralda handed me a cup of hot coffee as I sat myself in a chair opposite my host. She glanced at my reddened hand and made a nearly imperceptible smile.

"You weren't joshing about the winter around here," I stated flat-out.

"Well, this blow is much for this time of year. There'll be greater storms to come afore the winter has played out," he advised. He took a sip of coffee and leaned back in his chair just enough to not tip backward. "I dragged you in here to talk about Christmas. It's only a couple of days off."

"Already?" I asked.

"I likely neglected to share with you that we don't exchange gifts up here. Mostly, there aren't places close by to shop but more because we choose to celebrate Christ's birth with good eating and great song. Bottom line, Isa, I didn't want you worrying about gifts. I recall your pa and ma telling me that y'all celebrate that way."

I scanned the room. Running Waters was busy preparing something that resembled a side of beef, and there seemed to be a rather bountiful collection of vegetables and other foodstuffs that might be sufficient to feed an army. Esmeralda was busy helping her mother.

"Hap and Dred will be joining us for the celebration. Dred happens to possess a banjo, and Hap plays a mouth organ. Have you ever learned to play a musical instrument?"

I shook my head.

"Me neither, but it's time you learned. See that over there?" George pointed to a drape that outlined something large and box-shaped beneath it. He walked over and pulled away the drape. "One of the families in a recent wagon train found this contraption to be too heavy for the trail that lay ahead. The man of the family called it a piano. We managed to get it in here, but it's dreadfully out of tune." He plunked a few keys to demonstrate.

Sure enough, George stood alongside this upright piano. It was quite out of tune. I covered my ears at an especially discordant plunk of a key.

"I don't expect you to learn to play this thing in two days, but between us, we just might get it better tuned.

Worse case, we can make some cheery noise," he added with a laugh. "There's no one around to critique our music," he added, with a mischievous look.

"Oh, yes there is," pleaded Running Waters with a giggly laugh. "It will keep the Cheyenne and Lakota away. They will think bad spirits are here."

CHAPTER 6

CHRISTMAS

The blizzard let up on Christmas Eve. Gazing out the window, the sight we beheld under the warming rays of the sun caused the landscape to appear as though sprinkled with thousands of diamonds. Upon seeing it for the first time, you couldn't help but catch your breath at its incredible beauty. The snow cover spared nothing.

Early in the morning, I joined George, Hap, and Dred on a ride to those storm baffles that had been constructed for the livestock. Much to our delight, most of the herd had managed to find its way to the shelter. They'd in part been drawn to it by the lure of food.

"Well, that worked pretty doggone well, boys," observed George with breath that literally froze in the frigid air. "We'll have to build another for next winter." He knew that perhaps as many as thirty head hadn't sought the refuge, and many of those would be lost to the storm.

I shivered under my great buffalo coat and pined for the considerably milder Texas winter. "Great idea,

George. Do you reckon the storm baffle will become a habit for them?" I asked.

"They aren't especially stupid, Isa. They'll find their way here at first sign of the next storm," he replied. He scanned our surroundings. "Let's head out a mile or so and see whether there are any survivors we can save."

I was sort of incredulous given the temperature but understood George's concern. Hap and Dred offered no complaint, and off we rode.

* * *

After a couple of hours of riding horses that struggled to break through the crusting snow and accompanying drifts, we called it a day. We found a half dozen cattle and a horse frozen to death, but managed to herd two bulls, a cow, and three horses to the baffles and much-needed food. They'd recover in a couple of days and likely be wiser for the experience.

At the baffle, George turned to Hap and Dred. "See you boys tomorrow morning. Bring your appetites and be ready for a rip-roaring celebration." With that, he turned to me. "Let's finish up with that piano thing."

We gave the horses extra care in the barn before heading for the house. The cayuses sure deserved it. I must admit that I didn't ride Paint this day. I wasn't sure that he was quite ready to adapt to the climate. I promised myself that I'd take him for a walk later. I noticed Taabe acting strange. He was prancing back and forth with his ears perked up.

Hap and Dred had already cared for their horses, and George and I were about to leave the barn, when I heard something. It was a very weak moan that seemed to come from the far rear of the barn near a couple of hay bales. Taabe appeared anxious to investigate. "Did you hear that, George?"

He shook his head. "No."

"Something is back yonder," I stated. I began walking toward the spot from where the sound had come.

George grabbed his rifle, shrugged, and followed.

Assured by me, Taabe led the way. He wasn't growling, so I didn't expect any threat. Nevertheless, I did sweep back my coat and loosen the tie on my revolver.

Taabe began sniffing around the hay. Finally, he gave a low yelp as though having found something. In some respects, Taabe was like a hunting dog. He, of course, was far bigger and fearsome-looking than any hound.

I cautiously peered around the bale. There was a cradleboard covered in blankets. Beside it lay a woman. She looked to be a Lakota. She no longer breathed. The coldness of death had overtaken her. Somehow, she'd become lost in the storm, found her way to shelter, and had been unable to cling to life.

"Let's get her outside," advised George. "She'll freeze solid, and we can bury her at first thaw." This was a sad but true fact of life here in the cold wilds of the frontier. "You carry the baby to the house."

I was already hefting the cradleboard with the now-crying baby. Running Waters would know what best to do, so I hustled to get this foundling to the house.

"Running Waters, we found this baby in the rear of the barn along with its mother. She didn't make it. She looked to be a Lakota who became lost in the storm."

Running Waters was already unwrapping the baby from the cradleboard, and Esmeralda began warming something that looked to be milk, but I couldn't be sure.

"Boy or girl?" I asked.

"It's a boy child," said Running Waters with a nod and warm, loving smile.

George entered the house just as she made that announcement.

Taabe followed, seeming quite pleased with himself.

I watched as George and Running Waters looked long and thoughtfully at each other.

"The Lord taketh away, and He giveth," said George. He well knew what was on his wife's mind. "This child is His Christmas gift to us."

I found it to be an overwhelmingly emotional moment. I agreed with George that it was as though God was gifting them with a replacement for their son. It was their ultimate Christmas gift. There wasn't even a hint of a thought toward returning the baby to the Lakota.

"We must name him," uttered George through tear-filled eyes.

Running Waters held the baby close. "It is yours to say, husband."

George gazed thoughtfully into the fireplace as though turning prospective names over and over in his mind. Finally, he turned to Running Waters. "Zebediah," he stated firmly.

I knew the name translated to *gift from God*, as it was the name my pa had given to his wolf companion. Zeb was gone, but his name would live on with this very special gift to the Freemans.

At that, there was a rapping at the door, and Hap and Dred came barging in with their musical instruments. They must have been enhancing their joy back in the bunkhouse, as they were deliriously happy. This was going to be a Christmas celebration like no other that I'd ever experienced. "Yahoo!" I blurted. Shucks, I couldn't help myself. I looked around and everyone was filled with cheer. Aromas of food had begun to permeate the room, and everyone was in the spirit of Christmas.

We ate and ate and ate. Every time a plate emptied, someone replenished it. Delectables, coffee, and something known only to Hap and Dred were imbibed in prodigious quantities. We managed to roll from the dining table and sing a few songs. I plunked away at the piano, making plenty of noise but nothing that could be mistaken for music. Dred was a pretty fair banjo player, while Hap strung some melody together with his mouth organ.

We gathered at the hearth with George reading the Christmas story from the Bible. He stopped midway through, upon realizing that everyone had fallen asleep. We'd overindulged with food and spirit. Far as I could figure, it wasn't long before he joined the chorus of snoring and wheezing.

* * *

I can't say as winter was especially exciting, unless blizzards earn that appellation. We went out regularly to check livestock and to occasionally bring home some fresh meat. Three substantial storms struck. By substantial, I mean three or more feet of snow. Storms were invariably accompanied by strong winds. All in all, the toll on wildlife was heavy as deer and elk struggled in deep snow and predators sought the weakened prey. The storm baffle George had built mitigated any loss of beeves and horses.

I suppose the only time winter life got exciting was when we protected the livestock from those predators. Wolves and mountain lions found fresh-killed cattle a treat. Dred killed a mountain lion one morning that was going after a cow, and—with apologies to Taabe—Hap bagged a couple of wolves. I was grateful that Taabe didn't yield to his own baser instincts. Keeping him well-fed with fresh kill likely kept him on the straight and narrow. What we were unable to bring home, he found satisfaction for himself.

The first buds sprouted toward the beginning of April. These harbingers of spring gave us high hopes until winter threw one more storm at us. I was ever grateful for the warmth of the bunkhouse and the ranch house. I could only imagine what the famed mountain men must have experienced during winters among the rugged mountains of the frontier. That brought me to thinking about the Indians. I wondered what was cooking in their minds through the winter months. The onslaught of Whites certainly must have weighed heavily on their spirits. We did receive news that a homestead south of us had been struck by Southern Cheyenne. From what we heard, the Cheyenne were starving and attacked out of desperation.

We were all atwitter over the foundling Zebediah. The babe had been the center of attention, as even Hap and Dred doted over him. While it couldn't fill the cavernous hole left by the loss of their firstborn, George and Running Waters poured themselves into the child. I expect that even Esmeralda hadn't fully realized the depth of the loss of her brother until Zebediah joined the family, as she doted on the new addition to the family. Young Zebediah must have had God's blessing to have been found by the Freemans.

I did learn more about what life was like, when George and Running Waters first homesteaded out here on the North Platte River country. He told of living in a hut constructed of logs and sod for the first year until they could gather enough timber to build the first room of the ranch house. Over the years, they'd added rooms to the house, built out buildings and corrals, fenced pastures, and made other improvements.

CHAPTER 7

WAGON TRAIN ATTACKED

George and my discussion over breakfast focused on the wisdom of taking a look-see at Fort Laramie. We were curious as to whether the Army was regarrisoning the fort. Its strategic location on the Oregon Trail seemed unquestioningly important.

A wagon train had come lurching in last evening. It looked to be made up of about twenty wagons. They'd undoubtedly passed the fort and would know of its latest status. However, we were determined to venture out and see for ourselves.

We'd been dallying over coffee, when a shard of sunlight found its way through the partially parted drapes at one of the windows. Its near blinding light ricocheted off a knife and barely caught my eye.

George laughed. "I'll bet that's God saying we'd best get on with our day."

We bade Running Waters farewell, and I led the way outside. I'd no sooner set foot on the gallery boards than I heard distant shouting and gunshots coming from the direction of the North Platte. "George! Do you hear that?" I called out over my shoulder. I looked northward and could make out movement but not much else from nearly two miles away.

George had already ducked back inside to grab his rifle and warn Running Waters of the presence of hostiles.

I ran to the bunkhouse to fetch my own weapons. Hap and Dred were already awake and preparing for a day of checking pastures. "Y'all hear the commotion up on the river?"

Hap shook his head. "Isa, calm down. There's only four of us."

I gave him a questioning look.

"We must be ready to defend the Circled Cross in case the Indians get overconfident and head our way. No sense going out yonder and getting ourselves killed over a bunch of Injuns attacking circled wagons."

"We're not going to help them?" I pressed.

Hap and Dred shook their heads.

George entered the bunkhouse. "You men ready?" He looked at me. "You look disappointed, Isa."

I nodded.

"There are plenty of wagon trains that ramble through. If we helped defend them against every attack we've seen, we'd fast run out of ranch hands. We simply don't have enough force to help. Best we can do is defend ourselves. It's why the Army is out here."

"But?" I continued.

"After the fight, we'll mosey out there and see what we can do to help survivors. If the wagon train is well-led, they'll mostly survive. The Indians don't especially cotton to losing warriors unnecessarily."

The four of us left the bunkhouse with weapons in hand and ambled on over to the house where we sat on the gallery to listen to the battle. I found myself frustrated, but strove to understand George's logic. Actually, it made great sense so far as survival here on the frontier.

Running Waters and Esmeralda brought us coffee and sat with us as we listened to the battle. So far as we could make out, the Indians charged at least three times but were repelled. They surely coveted the horses and the cattle. The Whites were simply obstacles to their goal. We were like a cluster of distant spectators. We did see black smoke spiraling skyward from a wagon that had been set on fire.

I rather hoped that we'd hear the cavalry coming to the rescue, but that was unrealistic given that Fort Laramie was several hours distant. The hostiles surely knew that. By my guess, the attack had lasted about an hour. An eerie silence followed that battle. I looked to George with anticipation.

George simply watched the distant column of smoke.

We sat on the gallery for perhaps another twenty or thirty minutes until George stood. "Let's saddle up and see how they fared," urged George as he headed for the barn.

"Why'd we wait?" I asked.

George gave me a curious look. "The Indians might have still been close. No point in placing ourselves at risk. Oh, and it wouldn't have done to leave Circled Cross undefended."

I reflected on George's words. It was about risk out here. To let down your guard, to fail to anticipate, was to make yourself vulnerable. Death could be lurking around any bend in the trail.

We rode on out toward the wagon train. As we closed in on the circle of wagons, the heart-wrenching wails of some women broke the air. Men were shouting to care for the wounded while others were hauling buckets of water from the river to quench the wagon fire.

We must have been a sight riding up. A Black man leading a breed and two White cowboys.

A grizzled man carrying a Spencer rifle spotted us and exited the circle to confront us. "What be yer bizness?" he shouted. We were yet fifty or so yards out.

"George Freeman here. Y'all are camped on my ranch. Can we help?"

"Coulda used yuh thuty minutes ago," lamented the man. "Sol Hicks, heyah. I be the wagon boss."

"The Indians won't be back this day," assured George. "Our home is over yonder, if y'all have wounded needing special care."

"Thankee kindly. Might take yuh up on thet," responded Hicks. "This be the second attack in a week. Dang Injuns!" Hicks lowered his carbine and motioned us in.

"Any advice from Fort Laramie?" George asked as he dismounted.

"They be buildin' a post hospital and barracks. Whatcha call ironic, as they be puttin' thet hospital atop the old cemetery. It's gonna have twelve beds an' contain a kitchen, dinin' space, an' surgeon's office. Fancy dancy fer sure. Fort jus' needs more soldiers."

George shook his head. "How many wounded here, Mr. Hicks?"

"Nobody kilt. Ty Watt's wife took an arrow," responded Hicks. "Couple otha folks nicked."

Dred stayed with the horses, while George, Hap, and I entered the wagon circle. It wasn't as bad as I'd expected. The one wagon still smoldered. Minor wounds were already being patched up. Half a dozen folks were at what was apparently the Watts wagon. A couple of folks were on their knees seeing to Mrs. Watts' wound. It didn't look good, as an arrow had gone nearly through her chest. She struggled to breathe. Two youngsters were being held back. I gathered that they were her children. I found myself looking skyward and offering a prayer for her soul. It didn't help, as the women around her began crying, and Mr. Watts hugged his wife's lifeless form.

"Hey, look!" announced a rather strapping settler. "There be a Nigra an' a breed!"

George pivoted at the interjection of hateful prejudice and faced the man.

"Coyle! Stand down. These folks have offered help," responded Hicks with a nasty look at the man named Coyle.

"Lost my brother fightin' for them Nigras an' agin them Injuns." Coyle was getting heated. The blood on his forearm from a deep gash was evidence of having been engaged in fending off the hostiles. He spat toward George and me.

George simply stood silently. "Just trying to help, friend," he said calmly.

"You be no friend!" shouted Coyle as he took a couple of aggressive steps toward us.

"That's enough, Coyle!" ordered Hicks. Two men restrained Coyle.

"If y'all won't be needing our help, we'll be on our way." George maintained total calm. "Suggest your point man be extra alert as you head into yonder Laramie Mountains. Crazy Horse and Red Cloud are working up the Lakota to a lather. Y'all may have heard of the Fetterman Massacre."

"Fetterman?" queried Hicks.

"Yep. Just seven years back, Red Cloud and Crazy

Horse assembled nearly two thousand Lakota, Cheyenne, and Arapaho and wiped out Captain William Fetterman and his entire eighty-man detachment. It was right ugly, as I heard it, and not so far from these parts." George paused for effect. "So, be sure to keep a sharp lookout. I doubt they'll bring together two thousand warriors—yet—but they can do y'all some damage in the meantime."

Hicks's eyes widened. "Sure 'nuf appreciate the warning, Mr. Freeman."

We began to turn back toward Dred and the horses. George paused and pointed to a hill overlooking the North Platte. "If y'all need a spot to bury the woman, there are a few graves up yonder. Right peaceful spot."

Hicks nodded. "Thankee kindly, Mr. Freeman. Sorry 'bout Coyle."

George tipped his hat, and we rode off.

Another grave would nestle beside the Oregon Trail. It joined the human bones, discarded furniture, and burned-out wagons that marked its path.

* * *

Dred joined us as we all mounted up and headed back to the house.

"They were right lucky," I said to George as we rode off.

He rode silently for a few moments. "Lucky that Coyle fellow didn't tangle with us," he finally said. "It wouldn't have been pretty."

I wasn't inclined to inquire what George meant by *not pretty*. "Guess folks traveling from back east don't change their thinking much," I observed.

"You haven't hardly seen the worst of it, Isa," he

enjoined as he put his heels to his horse and charged ahead of us. I sensed that he was referring to me being half Comanche.

We didn't catch up to him until we reached the barn.

As we unsaddled our horses and curried them before setting them into the corral, George finally spoke up. "I don't have a good feeling about those folks up yonder," he said with a nod toward the wagon train. His characteristic smile was gone.

"Do you think the Lakota will return?" I pressed.

"Lakota…Shoshone…Cheyenne…could be any or all. I hear that General Sherman is of a mind to bend the will of the Indians through force. It'll be too late to save the folks on that wagon train." George hung his horse's bridle and washed his hands and face in the water bowl near the barn door. "Then again, maybe they'll be lucky." He hinted at a winsome smile, but his eyes were sad.

"My pa talked of him and Spirit Talker scouting for Texas Ranger Ford years back. Maybe I can meet this General Sherman." I reckoned I was likely drawing the short straw on my chances.

"You figure to scout? He's got plenty of scouts who know this country like the hairs on their chests," he chided.

"Guess I've got to get more familiar with the country. Then again, maybe my connection with Crazy Horse might come in handy."

George looked at me appraisingly. "Not a bad idea, Isa. Not a bad idea at all." He turned to Dred and Hap. "How about y'all get started on that second storm baffle. We heard from the Isa's pa, and he's planning to head some beeves our way. We sure don't want to lose any next winter."

"I'll be pleased to help," I offered.

"Appreciate that, but before you join Hap and Dred, let's grab some grub." George pressed his hat to his head against a strong breeze and headed off toward the house.

I shrugged and began to follow, when I realized Taabe was nowhere to be seen. Where had that critter gone off to? I reckoned he had picked up a scent and was answering his instincts, so I continued to follow George into the house.

* * *

"How were folks at the wagon train?" asked Running Waters as we strode in.

"Pig-headed," responded George as he poured himself some coffee. "But they'll likely make it to Oregon."

"Sit. We eat," directed Running Waters.

I followed George at the coffee pot. "How's Zebediah?" I asked in an attempt to break through a tightness I sensed in the room.

"He hungry, but Esmeralda feed him." That brought an inkling of a smile to Running Waters's lips, as it reminded her that her daughter was growing up. She laid a platter of venison slices and vegetables on the table before us.

George sighed. "One of the settlers made a stink about Isa and me. It was the usual Nigra and Indian thing that some of those eastern folks carry with them like some disease."

Running Waters looked off wistfully. It seemed as though she yearned for a wagon train free of prejudices. "Is sad," she said.

"Some folks are still fighting that danged war in their heads," I added. "Pa and Ma dealt with it after the war. Ma, being a Comanche, didn't set well with some. I recall

Pa telling me how Christ said you should love your neighbors like yourself. These prejudiced folks don't seem to love themselves, so likely wouldn't know the first thing about loving a neighbor."

"Your pa gave you good advice, Isa," responded George.

Esmeralda entered and joined us. "Zebediah sleep." She smiled at me a bit too friendly-like and earned a hint of a scowl from Running Waters.

"I met a girl at the Crazy Horse village," I said, thinking quickly. "Her name was Awentia, and she brought salves for my bruises. She was sweet."

Esmeralda looked down at her plate with a look of frustration and began eating.

I hoped there'd be someone here in the North Platte country for her. I knew that there were adjoining ranches. The escaped slaves my pa had brought up here on the cattle drive had established homesteads to raise livestock and farm the land. Wagon trains stopped at a wash off the North Platte just west of Fort Laramie to bathe and rest before tackling the Rocky Mountains, and some folks would surely decide to stay here. I took peace in feeling confident that Esmeralda would find a man to her liking and was sure George and Running Waters felt the same way. We could only hope she'd be patient and not be impulsive.

"You still up for a ride to Fort Laramie?" asked George.

"Tomorrow?" I asked.

"Yes. You should meet the garrison at the fort. It'll help if and when you ever meet General Sherman. Hap and Dred can keep watch while we're away." George paused and gave me one of those looks that said life would soon be getting quite interesting. Interesting would be an understatement. "The fort has changed since your pa last visited, especially with a hospital and new two-story barracks for the troops. Colonel David Stanley has just taken command. He's supposed to be heading an expedition out this summer to survey a route for the Northern Pacific Railroad along the Yellowstone River up north of here."

I recalled what I'd learned of the Fort Laramie Treaty with Red Cloud back in 1868, whereby the United States yielded to the chief's demand that the Bozeman Trail forts be abandoned. It also established the Great Sioux Reservation up in Dakota. It appeared to me that the expedition George described would place that treaty at considerable risk.

George continued. "He's got a mercuric second in command, a lieutenant colonel named George Armstrong Custer. He made quite a name for himself during the War Between the States for his gallantry and battlefield exploits."

"So Red Cloud's not supposed to be a problem?" I asked sort of rhetorically.

"Well, they recently brought the chief and a couple of other Sioux leaders to Washington and New York so they could better visualize the enormous resources and the huge population of Whites. You could say that was an awakening for the Indians." George looked off contemplatively at the Laramie Mountains. "But the onslaught of settlers and disease has been too much, and hostilities—much like you experienced—are increasing. The agents at the Red Cloud and Spotted Tail agencies are in serious danger. A side task of Colonel Stanley's survey is to verify the existence of large deposits of gold. If rumors are true, prospectors will swarm the reservation lands."

CHAPTER 8

SURPRISE

We rode out early, dipping our heads and lowering hat brims as we headed directly into the sun and followed the wagon ruts of the Oregon Trail. It was warming up quite nicely. Along with occasional showers the past couple of weeks, the land was ablaze with flowers and plenty of fresh leafy growth. The North Platte? The snows up in the distant mountains were beginning to melt enough to bring the river to full life.

We were enjoying the relaxing greenery and soothing whooshing sounds of the river. But for keeping an eye out for unwelcome company, most anyone seeing us would have thought we were out simply to enjoy our surroundings. However, appearances can be deceiving. We were headed up a little rise, when I pulled up. George reined in and looked over at me questioningly. I placed my finger against my lips.

It took another moment before George heard it too.

Our choices were decidedly limited. There was the river to our left, trees with dense undergrowth stood to our right, and there was the trail ahead and behind.

None of those options seemed worthy of consideration. My Comanche instincts took over as I
dismounted and squeezed Paint into the forest undergrowth. George followed as best he could, ducking
under some branches just as a band of Lakota rode into
view. That they passed us by in single file without
noticing our presence was amazing. I said a prayer, and
it apparently worked. The Lakota hadn't a clue as to
our presence.

We waited until the Lakota were out of sight. "That
was close," I whispered.

George nodded. "Wonder why they were so close to
Fort Laramie?"

I noticed that George was sweating just a bit. "You
okay?"

"Never know what those Lakota might be up to these
days," he said. "I counted eight warriors in the band,
likely scouting the fort." George looked over his shoulder
at me as I slipped the Spencer back into its scabbard.

I forced a smile. "A couple of them might have met
their Great Spirit," I whispered.

We led our mounts back onto the trail and resumed
our journey. I was pleased that we hadn't come up over
that rise and into the Lakota, as there was no telling how
they might have reacted. We stopped a couple of hours
shy of the fort and decided to cold camp near the river.
There was no point in going to the fort this late in
the day.

* * *

Up at the crack of dawn, we took as direct a route as
possible to the fort. As we crested a low hill, the strains
of Reveille reached our ears. "Praise God you don't have

that at the Circled Cross, George," I observed with a laugh.

We were a scant hundred yards from the entrance, when a company of cavalry came dashing out in a great flourish of jangling sabers and led by an officer who looked every bit their confident leader. This was my introduction to Lieutenant Colonel George Armstrong Custer. The Seventh Cavalry guidon flapped straight back in the wind as Custer led the company southward. I lamented that I would not be likely to meet him on this visit. I did take note that three Indians rode with him. I surmised that these were scouts.

"Crow," said George as he anticipated my question. We watched Custer ride off on what was likely a training exercise. "Shall we go and get acquainted with Colonel Stanley?"

We headed for the headquarters. As we rode in, I noted a sense of certain tension among the soldiers we saw. It was a tension spawned by their upcoming expedition to the Yellowstone country. Any journey into the unknown was fraught with great uncertainties and the ever-present prospect of dangerous encounters. I watched Custer's detail fade into the distance. I'd heard of his exploits battling Indians after the war. He'd served under Major General Winfield Scott Hancock in fighting the Cheyenne and dealt with the aftermath of a massacre whereby Lieutenant Lyman Kidder, ten troopers, and a scout on their way to deliver dispatches to General Sherman and Custer were wiped out by Lakota and Cheyenne. Custer went on to establish Camp Supply from which, under General Sheridan's orders, he led an attack on Black Kettle's Cheyenne encampment on the Washita River. I reckoned there must have been a sense of vengeance at work, as Custer killed more than a hundred and fifty warriors, women, and children, and took no prisoners. They killed nearly nine hundred captured Indian ponies.

Now, Custer found himself at Fort Laramie preparing to ostensibly protect a railroad survey party on the Yellowstone River.

"Isa," called out George. "You coming?"

I'd been sort of mesmerized with thoughts of Custer's adventures on the frontier. "Yes, I'm coming," I replied with one more look off at the dust where Custer's troopers had fallen beneath the horizon.

"You should know that the colonel served as a Union general during the war. He was awarded the Medal of Honor for bravery."

"How come he's a colonel now, and no longer a general?" I asked.

"Well, he was injured and left the service for a brief time. I'm sure stars are in his future," responded George.

We climbed the stairs leading to Colonel Stanley's office.

"Halt, who goes?" demanded the corporal standing guard.

"Morning, Fred," replied George. "Just here to meet your latest commanding officer." It was apparently a sort of running joke at the near-constant changes of command at Fort Laramie. "This here is Isa O'Toole. He's one of Jack O'Toole's sons."

Fred nodded friendly-like. He was one of the infantrymen who'd been around for a couple of years, having been promoted or demoted over behavior issues every couple of months. "Oh sure, Mr. Freeman. Let me check. The colonel is a tad feisty this mornin'," he said, with a wink, and then ducked inside.

I gathered expeditions into hostile Indian territory

just might cause a bit of feistiness in some folks as an outlet for tension. I thought he might find some peace of mind with a bit of Bible reading and a dose of prayer.

"Colonel Stanley will be pleased to make yer acquaintance, gents," offered Fred upon emerging from the office.

We walked into Stanley's office and found him standing at the window watching as a parade formation. The office was dark and had a mustiness to it, but the colonel seemed all spit and polish. He extended his hand as he turned to greet us. He appeared momentarily taken aback at seeing a Black man and half-breed standing before him.

"Pleasure to meet you, Mr. Freeman, Mr. O'Toole. The corporal said you own a ranch west of here." Stanley pointed to a couple of chairs and took a seat behind the gnarled old oak desk the Army had issued to the fort. He chose a cigar from a thermidor on the desk. "You care for a smoke?"

George shook his head. "Thanks, Colonel, but we'll pass." This young man here is the son of a rancher friend of mine down Texas way. Despite his youth, Isa O'Toole here has already had experience fighting *pistoleros* on his pa's ranch and has parleyed with Crazy Horse."

George was laying it on a bit thick to say I parleyed with the Lakota chief, but who was I to argue.

Stanley nodded a tad condescendingly as though wondering what this had to do with him. He shuffled some papers, as if to indicate he had better things to do.

"I hear tell you are heading up to the Yellowstone." George glanced at me. "How are you fixed for scouts, Colonel?"

Stanley's eyes widened, and he immediately looked

up. "You offering this wet behind the ears boy as a scout?"

I was as surprised as the colonel. George had never mentioned this to me. Of course, the image of riding off on an adventure with Custer sat well in my imagination.

"Buffalo Hump, the Penateka Comanche chief, was his grandfather. His father is near legendary as a hunter and Indian fighter in Texas. In fact, Jack O'Toole scouted for Texas Ranger Captain Ford back at Little Robe Creek. Isa speaks Comanche and a little Lakota, is a fine hunter, and would serve you well, Colonel."

"What do you think, O'Toole? You up for some scouting?" asked Stanley.

I was in a bit of shock. It was reassuring that Stanley apparently held no prejudices against Blacks or half-breeds. The prospect of scouting for the expedition was simply too good to pass up. My youthful mind conjured up all sorts of adventure. "Er..." I stole a glance at George, who gave me a nod. "Yes, Colonel, sir. Yes." I had monumental difficulty trying to remain calm.

"We'll be leaving in a few days, Mr. O'Toole. I suggest that you talk with our supply officer to be sure you're properly equipped." The colonel pulled out a sheet of paper and scrawled what appeared to be orders. He stopped mid-stroke. "How old are you, son?"

I couldn't lie. "Sixteen, sir."

"That's a bit too young for this man's army. I'm afraid..."

"Sir? If you would consider how much faster young men grow up out here. Why, if Isa were with the Comanche, he'd be joining war parties in battle. He's already proven himself in fights." George quickly came to my defense.

Colonel Stanley gave me a once-over to size me up. "I can't give you any government-issue equipment, son."

"I have my pony, Spencer carbine, bow and arrows, knife, and Colt revolver, sir." I didn't tell him about Taabe.

"We'll get you most of what you'll need back at the ranch, Isa," assured George.

The colonel tore up the paper he'd been writing on and began a new note. "You just show this to any trooper that challenges you, Isa. I'll inform Lieutenant Colonel Custer myself. You should be aware that he has a favorite scout from the Crow tribe."

I recalled that the Comanche and Crow weren't exactly allies, but that was long ago. "I can handle it, sir."

"You get what you need from George here. When you return, I'll introduce you to Lieutenant Colonel Custer." Stanley reached out his hand, and we shook. "I've heard of your pa, son. Fine man. I read what turned out to be his letters against slavery that were published back east." He smiled and stood. That was the signal that our meeting had ended.

We gave what we hoped appeared to be snappy salutes and departed.

Once outside, George reined me in. "It's not going to be easy, Isa. There are plenty of Indian haters among the troops. They'll try to make you do menial tasks. Don't fall for it. You're big and strong. Don't be afraid to defend yourself."

I set my jaw and gazed into George's eyes. "I can handle it," I assured him. I knew fighting experienced soldiers would be quite a bit more challenging than fights with my brothers. To say that I was surprised at the opportunity to accompany the Yellowstone Expedition would be a gross understatement. I was surprised and thrilled. "Let's get back to the ranch and make sure I have what I'll need." I intuitively figured I'd have to carry all my own gear, since I wasn't officially a member of the Army.

* * *

I was bursting at the seams to share the news with Hap and Dred, but especially with Running Waters and Esmeralda. As we pulled up to the barn, Hap and Dred were leaning against the corral fence with knowing smiles. Apparently, George was planning this all along. "You knew!" I blurted.

Hap couldn't stop laughing. "Gonna be a rip-roarin' adventure, son."

Dred simply nodded. "Go on in the house an' grab some grub, Isa. We'll take care of Paint here."

I smiled as Dred stepped close to Paint to grab his halter and nearly had his hand bitten. "He's a one-man pony," I warned. "I'll see to him." I began to lead Paint into the barn but paused. "Y'all seen Taabe?"

Hap laughed. "Oh yeah," he chortled. "He got hisself a woman."

It sounded as though my dear wolf companion would now have divided loyalties. Family did come first. I wondered if and when I'd meet the bride. I headed for a stall. Paint would need good food and rest before we ventured to the Yellowstone.

George followed. "I wonder whether Stanley and Custer will tolerate your wolf friend?" he pondered.

I thought on that. It hadn't come up in our conversation with the colonel. "I reckon it'll be a right large contingent of men and equipment. If I'm doing my job, I mostly won't be near them. I doubt I can keep Taabe and his mate totally away, but I'll try best I can. After all, Taabe and I are partners."

As we emerged from the barn, there stood Taabe and the prettiest female wolf I'd ever laid eyes on. Of course, he was considerably larger, but she appeared to be the perfect partner.

Taabe padded over and nuzzled my hand.

Hap and Dred looked on and shook their heads. They still hadn't figured out how I had forged a relationship with a wolf. It defied all they knew.

But a moment later, Taabe's mate came over, hesitated, and following his example, nuzzled my hand. The bond with her was now forged.

Hap and Dred were fully amazed. "Dang!" they exclaimed in near unison.

"Let's go get some grub," urged George with one of his broad grins.

"Wait. I must name her," I called out.

"Give it some thought, Isa." He chuckled. "Taabe may want a say."

Taabe and his mate followed us into the house, where we were greeted with hugs and exclamations of joy at our safe return. Of course, I was quick to share my surprise news.

CHAPTER 9

YELLOWSTONE EXPEDITION

Upon arriving at Fort Laramie, I learned that we'd be heading out the next morning to Fort Rice up in the Dakota Territory. The plan was to join the 353-person survey team and six companies under Major Townsend of the Ninth Infantry that would depart Fort Abraham Lincoln on the Missouri River a few days earlier. The full expedition would depart on June 23, 1873.

To say I was excited would be a gross understatement. It didn't take me long to be fully impressed with the undertaking. Colonel Stanley's column was to be comprised of more than 1,530 cavalry and infantry, two artillery pieces, sixty days of rations, 275 mule-drawn wagons, and twenty-seven Indian and mixed-blood scouts. I reckoned that I was among the latter, though I was too young to be enlisted.

I was sitting at dinner beside an infantry sergeant who had taken me under his wing, apparently on orders from the colonel, and had the temerity to ask what the expedition expected to encounter.

"Them Injuns under Sitting Bull have about a thousand warriors that include his own Hunkpapas under the War Chief Rain in the Face, plenty of Oglalas under Crazy Horse, and a few Miniconjou and Cheyenne," shared Sergeant Rawls, between chews on an especially tough chunk of brisket.

"Appears that we outnumber them," I observed.

Rawls chuckled. "Question is, can we outfight them?" Rawls had been laying appraising eyes on me since my arrival. He seemed a reasonable fellow and held no special animosity toward Indians. He was a professional soldier to his core. "The word is out that all the Indian scouts are to wear a white band around their heads so they don't suffer from friendly fire in any battle."

I recalled my pa telling me that the Tonkawas and other tribal scouts under Texas Ranger Captain Ford at the Battle of Little Robe Creek wore white headbands. In the heat of battle, they tossed them aside, as they became marked men for the Comanche. It appeared that the Yellowstone Expedition was going to make the same mistake. "Wearing a white band might tend to make us targets for any enemy," I observed.

Rawls nodded. "Guess it's a choice of who you want shooting at you." He chortled. "Sort of ironic, isn't it?" He savored a long sip of coffee. "You seem pretty bright, Isa. Seems you've packed a bit of experience in that young head of yours." He gave me a head-to-toe scan as we sat. I was wearing buckskins, moccasins, and a broad-brimmed felt hat. "That pinto pony of yours stands out like a sore thumb. If you're worried about a white headband, you might think on that horse."

I smiled easily. "Reckon those Sioux might think I'm one of them, Sergeant."

"Maybe," responded Rawls. "I understand you're

packing a bow and quiver of arrows along with your guns and knife. You're dang-well outfitted. Likely more than most of the infantry under the colonel's command and surely more than any Sioux."

"Is that a problem?" I asked.

"I think the colonel has it in mind to keep you close to the column. To me, that seems a waste. I'll see to getting you well out in front where you can keep an eye out for any threats." Rawls leaned back and scratched his chin in thought. "What brought you up to Fort Laramie, Isa?"

I shared my story, emphasizing the accomplishments of my pa.

"So, you were raised under a Christian roof with what the Indians might call the White man's values and teachings," Rawls observed. "Heck of a fine testament to your folks," he added admiringly.

"I reckon I'll get back home in due time," I replied.

"What about those wolves?"

I figured that my companions were lurking somewhere in the sergeant's mind. It was a logical question to ask, and he was likely asking on behalf of others who were curious. Stanley had put out an order to leave Taabe and his mate be, that they were part of the expedition. "I'm not sure you'll understand, Sergeant, but I'll try. The male appeared by my side during my vision quest. He is the offspring of a wolf that adopted my pa. He named it Zebediah, which means gift from God. It served to enhance Pa's image among any Indians he encountered. Keep in mind that the wolf is strong medicine and is venerated by many tribes for its leadership qualities. My companion's name—Taabe—is the Comanche word for sun, the image of the great spirit. Now, Taabe has found a mate. There's no accounting for their presence or why Taabe latched on to me, other than he is some working of God."

Rawls nodded. "Amazing. If I hadn't seen it, I would never believe it. I expect they're right protective of you?"

I smiled. "Pretty much." I glanced out the window past Rawls to heightened activity on the parade ground as men and equipment were still being assembled. "Looks as though we'll pull out on schedule, Sergeant."

"The colonel is a stickler for being on schedule. I've got some duties to attend to," he said with a smile as he arose. "You stay out of trouble. Take my advice and get away from the main column as much as you can. There are some who don't take kindly to anyone with Indian blood running in their veins…even those on our side."

I shook Rawls's hand and followed him out.

* * *

Well, I mostly got my wish as I ventured ahead of the column with two Crow scouts and a part Pawnee half-breed. They were all older than me and didn't seem inclined to let me forget that fact. The scouts spoke broken English, so communication was challenging.

The age problem was quickly solved on the third day of the march, when we had stopped to rest our horses. I had a gut feeling that something wasn't right. One of the Crows had decided to sit a spell and wasn't paying atten-tion to his surroundings. From my right, Taabe appeared with the hind end of a bobcat in his jaws. They were headed at the Crow scout. It all happened in a flash. I swung my Spencer carbine in time to put a round into the bobcat. The bobcat and wolf plowed into the scout, and he found himself alive but lying on the ground with a dead feline and hungry wolf on top of him. He pushed his way to his feet and watched Taabe finish off the feline.

"Cat stalk you? I saw him just as wolf attack. Wolf save your life," I said in English, I hoped he'd understand.

The Crow scout was still frightened and had a long gash from a bobcat claw on his arm, but was otherwise unscathed. He gave me a look that said he was forever in my debt.

The other two scouts stood back, shaken but beginning to appreciate what had just happened. They looked at Taabe with some trepidation until I motioned that they were safe. They went to the aid of the Crow scout while Taabe began enjoying a meal of bobcat.

After finishing their meal, Taabe and his mate padded over to me. Taabe offered me a bobcat haunch. I figured it best not to refuse a gift, especially from a wolf. I took it and stood for a moment with it. Taabe stared at me with his big blue wolf eyes as though urging me to eat. My fellow scouts watched me with eager anticipation. Finally, I bit a chunk of sinewy meat from the haunch. I chewed, swallowed, and wiped my bloodied chin. Taabe poked at me with his wet nose and led his mate away.

The Pawnee scout knew a little Comanche. "*Sunipu*," he stated. "Much *sunipu*."

This was the Comanche word for medicine, and I suppose the scouts reckoned I had a lot. White men might have said that I had a lot of sand. Courage? Strong medicine? Shucks, I reckoned it was about God.

We rode on for another five miles before getting word that the expedition was halting for the night. The follow-up news was less welcome. The surveying party and its escort under Major Townsend had been seriously delayed by rain and a bad hail storm in which some men felt they might be killed by stampeding animals. Several wagons were destroyed, and Stanley sent Custer and the Seventh Cavalry to help repair the damage. The expedition was further delayed as Stanley sent nearly fifty wagons back to Fort Rice for more supplies.

The incident left us scouts waiting patiently under a clear starlit sky. I saw Taabe and his mate silhouetted against the full moon. I smiled to myself. I decided to call her Mua. I had the sun and the moon as my wolf companions. If my vision quest was being fulfilled, the journey sure was to my liking. I did wonder how my brothers and sister were doing back at Rising Cross Ranch. Pa was surely keeping them busy. If a trail drive was planned, would they come with the drive?

* * *

By July 5, Townsend and the survey team had caught up with Stanley's column. We pushed on, entering the Montana Territory and reaching the Yellowstone a week later. The rivers were high, but we managed to cross them as necessary.

I watched as Custer led away a couple of squadrons of cavalry to meet a steamboat near the mouth of what they called Glendive Creek on the Yellowstone River. Apparently, a supply depot was being established. Upon his arrival, Colonel Stanley left two Seventh Cavalry companies and a Seventeenth Infantry company to guard the depot.

We continued westward, reaching the Powder River and another steamboat around August 1. There was talk of Indians having been spotted and a couple of minor skirmishes. Next morning, we continued along the Yellowstone. The two Crows, Pawnee breed, and myself were forming a team of sorts. We all knew that we were being watched and had been long before the discovery near the Powder River.

Owing to the incident with the bobcat, I sensed that my companions had begun to look upon me as a sort of leader of our party. My strong *sunipu* had impressed them.

* * *

Little did I know that Crazy Horse himself was following the expedition. He was likely puzzled by the machinations of the surveyors with their equipment and measurements. I held little doubt that he realized that this portended the influx of many more settlers.

Stanley had us encamped along a hill near the mouth of Sunday Creek, a tributary of the Yellowstone. Captain Yates of the Seventh Cavalry led a company guarding the work of the surveyors. Custer was off scouting with two companies.

I was far upriver so wouldn't know it, but one of the Sahiyela people among the Lakota recognized the unit markings of soldiers under Custer that had killed many of Black Kettle's Cheyenne along the Washita River just a few years back. The warrior was so angry that he charged across the river and ran into heavy fire from the soldiers. Custer's men dismounted and formed a skirmish line. The bank along the river served as a natural parapet to fend off attack.

The battle went on for about three hours in heat that I guessed to be well over a hundred degrees. Crazy Horse pulled the warriors back when he saw what he called the wagon gun, the cannon Stanley had brought. Custer had finally had enough of the siege tactics. He charged from the defenses and scattered the Lakota, pursuing them upriver.

Crazy Horse tried to decoy the soldiers into an ambush, but they drew back before reaching the spot chosen for the ambush. Frustrated and with ammunition running low, Crazy Horse wisely called off the attack. I'm sure the chief returned to his lodge with deep troubles on his mind. The settlers kept coming, the cottonwoods weren't so plentiful, elk and deer were harder to find, and the buffalo herds were dwindling. A coughing sickness had invaded his camp. Like I'd heard from soldiers, a hard winter was expected. Everyone will be laying in supplies to endure. He was likely not yet aware that the Red Cloud's people were to be moved far to the north, much to the old chief's chagrin.

Had I known of the incident, called the *Battle of Honsinger's Bluff* by Stanley, I would have liked to have been there and perhaps had the prospect of again meeting the wise and mighty Tasunke Witko.

Stanley never flinched as the expedition moved on.

* * *

A couple of days after the fight with the Lakota, me and my scout companions took a well-earned break from our duties and headed into camp. I decided to find Sergeant Rawls. It turned out to not be so easy.

"Hey! Lookee thar. Injuns an' breeds!" hollered a trooper to his half-drunk friends. I wanted to tell them that they were alive thanks to us and the two dozen other scouts on the expedition.

I led us past the taunters.

"Whar yuh goin'? Yuh yella bellies!" The trooper was showing off for those willing to listen. They'd been on the trail for more than a month, and the long days and nights were showing their effect.

I was bent on ignoring the man.

"Yep, yella bellies fer sure!" he continued. Then, he threw a stone that hit Paint in the neck. He reared a little in surprise. "Horse yella, too!"

Hitting Paint was too much. I slid from my saddle. I was at least four inches taller and fifty pounds heavier than the trooper.

The trooper saw my revolver and knife, focused in on the bear claws around my neck, and looked up at me with his mouth now gaping. His friends began laughing and goading him on.

"Knives or fists?" I challenged. I knew I could handle either. "And can I have your scalp when we're finished?" Pa had taught me a bit about intimidating a potential foe.

The trooper gave me a curious look as his liquor-induced confidence waned.

"And can my wolf friend eat you after that?" I was fully laying on the intimidation.

Now, the trooper saw Taabe and Mua sitting beside Paint. "Er, I dint mean nothin'."

"You owe my friends an apology," I demanded calmly.

The trooper's companions were no longer laughing. "Yuh better say yer sorry, John," they urged.

John apologized reluctantly.

I gave a warm smile to the troopers, mounted, and rode on. My fellow scouts were as amazed as the troopers.

Man Who Hunts, the Pawnee breed whom I'd saved from the bobcat, shook his head. "Never seen anything quite like that, Isa. You sure you're only sixteen?"

We finally reached the tent of Sergeant Rawls with only one other slightly less confrontational encounter.

* * *

Rawls sat in front of his tent with three other troopers from the Seventh Cavalry. Rawls was nursing a wound from a bullet that had grazed his upper arm.

"Hail the camp!" I called as a matter of formality.

"Get yourself in here, Isa. Your friends, too," replied Rawls.

The three troopers sat with mouths agape at the four of us.

"Don't mind them," assured Rawls. "I expect y'all watched the little fight up near the Little Bighorn at Pease Bottom. The Seventh lost a couple of good men, but Sitting Bull's warriors were run off. I don't know how much longer the tribes can fight. Their fate is sealed."

"Do you think it's God's desire?"

"Don't know how God plays in this. The outcome looks pretty much inevitable," he observed. "But we're already yakking too much. Set a spell and pour some coffee."

We sat for the next couple of hours sharing our experiences thus far on the Yellowstone Expedition. I expect I should consider myself fortunate to have experienced so few challenges along the journey. The bobcat and dealing with bullies were about all. We saw Indians from afar, but never engaged with any. For me, I was especially taken in by the majestic scenery, the wildlife, and the clear mountain air. We did shoot elk and deer, so we dined well.

We bade Rawls farewell in the morning. It was but a couple of days later that we were called in from our scouting position and informed that the expedition was complete and would be heading back down the Yellow-stone River.

The experience with the expedition left me wondering at what outcome God had in mind for my vision quest. Pa had assured me that it would be an obvious call to some purpose. I expect I'd matured quite a bit for this experience. I also realized that it would be October when I got back to the Circled Cross near Fort Laramie. It looked likely that I'd be spending another winter enjoying George's hospitality. What might it bring?

As the column lumbered slowly along on its return to Fort Rice, I decided that it made sense to depart for Fort Laramie early. About the time we reached a place along the Yellowstone called Clark's Fork Bottom, which featured a sawmill and a growing population, I parted company with my scout companions. Since I wasn't a full-fledged soldier, I enjoyed more decision-making flexibility. I rode to Sergeant Rawls's tent and shared my decision.

"Sergeant, I think it's time we parted company. At the pace the expedition is going, we could see the first snow before any of us got back to Fort Laramie." I made my case as briefly as I figured was necessary.

"You're likely making a good decision, and I don't doubt that you can travel back to the fort alone." He gave an eye to Taabe and Mua, knowing I had strong company. "I'll let Colonel Stanley know, Isa."

The expedition had been pretty much uneventful for me, especially as I'd missed the battle with Crazy Horse. "I've appreciated your advice, Sergeant Rawls."

"You handle yourself right well, Isa." He was referring to my dustups with troopers over my being a half-breed. "Stay alert as you head home. Oh, and see the cookie for supplies." Rawls stood and gripped my hand. In the dim light of early evening, I thought I spotted a tear or two in this rugged soldier's eyes. "God be with you, son," he said as he turned and disappeared into his tent.

I stood there pondering the moment before heading to the cookie to draw some supplies. I'd head southward in the morning.

CHAPTER 10

THE QUEST CONTINUES

The journey southward was picturesque to say the very least. Paint, my wolf companions, and I were now seasoned travelers of the frontier. An upside of that was that we were far more trail-wise. I must admit that I had fallen into a little pridefulness at having scouted for the famous David Stanley and George Custer. I wasn't clueless as to the possibility of that experience paying off later. Meanwhile, my vision quest continued. It was beginning to feel as though it might go on forever.

I gave Paint his head so long as it was in a generally southward direction. Taaba and Mua would come and go at will. It occurred to me that there'd likely be wolf pups soon enough. Would Taabe hang around like Pa's Zeb, or leave? How deeply did loyalty run?

I admit to missing home. What were George, Peter, and little Nadua up to? How were Ma and Pa? The bass were likely biting on the Guadalupe River, and the Rising Cross Ranch was surely flourishing. If Pa was going to drive a herd up to Fort Laramie, would he lead or put Shorty in charge? I guess I wouldn't know until I found my way back to the Freemans' spread. There could be a letter. Okay, the biggest admission I must make as I traveled with only myself to converse with is that I found my thoughts drifting to Morning Star. She sure was a pretty girl. I wondered whether she was spoken for. Comanche girls married young, and the same was likely for the Lakota. I guessed she was thirteen or fourteen years old. Would I ever see her again? Living in the camp of Crazy Horse meant that, if I ever did see her again, it might not be under the most pleasant circumstances.

My biggest concern remained the question of where God was pointing me. Where was this vision quest headed?

I made camp beside a small stream. I figured it was likely a tributary to the Yellowstone River. The water ran clean across its rocks, and the sun's light reflected upon it such that it looked to be sprinkled with precious gems. This sure was beautiful country.

The cookie had supplied me with plenty of jerky. I had made some pemmican using my ma's recipe, so you might say that I enjoyed a balanced diet. I even heated up some coffee. I was determined to acquire some fresh meat, as a regular diet of jerky would get old in a hurry.

* * *

I thought Paint might be getting tired of me babbling about the scenery and life in general. I even pulled out the Bible Pa had given me and read verses now and again. If Paint could talk, he might well become a preacher, if good book learning was all it took. Taabe and Mua came and went, though I expected to see pups one of these days.

I'm not sure what possessed me to ride with the Spencer across my lap. Perhaps, I wanted to be ready if the right prey came into view. Then again, I felt a strange sensation this morning. It was telling me that danger lurked. I began doing a bit of back-trailing. It slowed me down, but I was concerned about being followed. I shouldn't have been. The threat was ahead of me and was likely looking to find the perfect spot to ambush me.

I posed fairly attractive prey for a warrior looking to count coup. My weapons and horse alone were valuable. I'd just be an inconvenience to any attacker.

Paint was picking his way among rocks and scrub pine when I looked down trail to see three Indians about a hundred and fifty or so yards distant. I wasn't certain, but they looked to be Lakota. If three were in view, there were at least twice that number lurking nearby.

The Lakota in the center looked familiar, but was yet too far away to be sure of his identity. They'd seen me, so there was no point in delaying the inevitable. I said a prayer to myself and nudged Paint along.

They waited. Their ponies pranced a bit with a few snorts and whinnies. Two more warriors joined the three. They were armed to the teeth and painted up right well. It was obvious that they sought human prey rather than animal.

As I rode another fifty yards closer, I finally recognized Buffalo Man. He was a long way from Crazy Horse's encampment. Taabe and Mua padded along beside me. For any warriors unfamiliar with Isa O'Toole and his acquaintanceship with their chief, Crazy Horse, I must have presented quite a sight. My six-foot-three frame was decked out in my fringed buckskins with high-top moccasins and tan flat-brimmed hat. My weaponry surely got their attention, as in addition to the

Spencer rifle across my lap, they couldn't miss the Colt revolver in my holster and my bow and quiver of arrows. But the bear claw necklace coupled with my wolf escort spoke volumes as to the strong *sunipu* I gave off. I was not some wayfarer to be trifled with.

I saw Buffalo Man speaking animatedly to his warriors. Apparently, I was under some sort of protection of Crazy Horse.

Tathanka raised his rifle high over his head, then brought it down and made a sign of peace over his chest. He motioned me forward.

I'd shot a young doe that morning, and it was draped across Paint's rump. It looked as though I was about to share it.

"*Wowahwa*, Isa Comanche," said Tathanka.

"Tathanka," I responded. "*Ana o'a hi'it*," I said, motioning to the doe behind me and then making a sweeping motion of my open hand to the warriors with Buffalo Man.

The Lakota responded with smiles. There was a creek with plenty of running water, but a few feet away, so the warriors dismounted to build a fire and enjoy my invitation.

I suppose there's little that can bring souls together like food, and roasted venison was very much on the menu. I broke out some of my pemmican as I sat around a campfire with ten war-painted but laughing Lakota.

I was amused by the occasional somewhat-fearful looks that crossed the faces of the warriors, as Taabe and Mua laid beside me gnawing on raw venison. I must admit that such a sight would be intimidating to most folks. It surely had the Lakota buzzing over whatever strong *sunipu* I possessed. If I'd told them that I had nothing to do with the wolves' presence and that it was a

God thing, it might have destroyed the aura that hung over the current circumstances. I wished I had the courage or could create an open discussion of faith, but I'd likely be pushing my luck. Perhaps, I could meet one-on-one at some later time with Tathunka. This definitely was not the time to be challenging Lakota beliefs.

Buffalo Man and I talked mostly in sign with a mix of Lakota, Comanche, and English thrown in. He had been watching the Yellowstone Expedition in its travels and was curious as to its intentions. He animatedly signed that he'd battled the Blue Coats and Yellow Hair, the name they had bestowed upon Custer. "Tasunke Witko *kize wasichus*." He puffed out his chest with pride and made it clear that Crazy Horse himself had led the Lakota.

I tried to explain that a railroad was coming, and I think they understood. I drew my best impression of railroad tracks in the dirt beside the fire. I must have been a sight trying to depict a huge locomotive belching steam and pulling passenger cars. Importantly, they appeared to grasp that more Whites would follow.

Buffalo Man told me that Sitting Bull and Crazy Horse were beginning to talk of a great gathering of tribes a few moons off. They would camp near a river that Whites called the Little Bighorn. They called the place Greasy Grass and planned to defend their hunting grounds against the Whites. Then, he gave me a curious look, and partly in sign, asked, "Isa *wasichus*?" He had seen me at the head of the expedition column and wanted to know why I rode with the White men.

How might I best answer? The Lakota words that might explain it were unknown to me. As I wrestled with this challenge, it occurred to me that an answer was at hand. I signed in great sweeping motions that it was part of my vision quest, and that I sought to better understand the purposes of the *wasichus*.

Buffalo Man nodded as though he understood. He repeated the hand motions I used to describe the vision quest and nodded again. The vision quest was a revered act, so my having been led by the Great Spirit excused my being with the expedition. Of course, he didn't understand that my Great Spirit, my Comanche *Taa Narumi*, was God.

I consciously didn't share with Buffalo Man that the Yellowstone Expedition was also looking for deposits of the yellow metal. There would be far more Whites greedily coming into land supposedly set aside by the Fort Laramie Treaty of 1868. The Lakota couldn't possibly imagine the great numbers of *wasichus* that would pursue gold. Many would die on both sides.

As we extinguished the fire and finished the last of the venison and most of my pemmican, I grasped Buffalo Man's hand. *"Kola,"* I said in the Lakota tongue, which translates to *friend*. I think Buffalo Man appreciated that I was using his language.

"Kola," he responded. He looked me straight in the eyes, nodded with a smile, and then mounted his war pony.

I hoped and prayed that we would indeed remain friends. It may have been in God's hands, but I'd do all I could to foster it. Imprinted forever in my subconscious were God's words in Genesis 1:28 to subdue the earth and extract its potential. For me, here and now, that extended to planting seeds of friendship, the bounty of which might later be reaped.

I watched the war party head out. They were an impressive band decked out in their feathered finery with decorated bone breastplates, shields, and lances, along with bows and arrows and a couple of rifles. They hadn't mentioned any particular target they sought to attack, though I reckoned that with only ten warriors, it was likely to be easy pickings. It could be a small homestead or an enemy hunting party. No matter whom they attacked, suicide was never an option. Good warriors were hard to replace. I felt blessed to have encountered Buffalo Man, since the outcome with a war party of a tribe unknown to me might have ended quite unpleasantly for me.

I now proceeded with increased caution. I was just about halfway to George's spread, which meant that I still had nearly a week's travel ahead. I didn't figure to press my luck in any more encounters. I strove to focus my thinking, to pay greater attention to my surroundings, and to backtrail occasionally as my pa had taught us. Back-trailing meant slower progress but greater safety from attack. I had what folks called apex predators to worry about, too. Taabe and Mua offered some protection, and Paint was ever-sensitive to unusual stirrings along our path.

* * *

I pushed Paint hard. Taabe and Mua still followed along, though they galavanted off now and then to do whatever wolves do. Taabe was big as wolves go, every bit the image of Zeb.

I soon found myself nearing the headwaters of what I figured to be the North Platte River. This meant that I was about five days from the Circled Cross Ranch. September was drawing to a close, and it wouldn't be long before the leaves would turn in their colorful glory and the temperatures would drop. Another couple of months, and my breath would form a fog before me. The prospect made me chuckle involuntarily. This sure enough was a long way from my Texas roots.

We were traveling at a good pace when Paint swerved to avoid a fallen tree. Suddenly, his ears went forward, and he began acting a tad distressed. This was concerning, as I saw no rattlesnake or other critter that might be a threat. A short distance ahead of us, Taabe and Mua seemed very stressed. I pressed my heels into Paint's sides to hurry him along despite his upset, and we quickly broke into a clearing just beyond the fallen tree. Taabe was whimpering and darting back and forth at something under a bush. I rode closer and slipped from the saddle to investigate. I walked cautiously toward the spot with my hand on the grip of my Colt revolver as a precaution. Sadly, the distress was about a dead wolf. An arrow protruded from its side. I stood helplessly as Taabe and Mua mourned the poor fellow. From the look of it, the wolf had been shot hours ago. No telling what had become of whoever shot him. "I'm sorry, Taabe. I can't help him." Of course, there was no comfort a human could offer a wolf.

Mua sniffed the air and began to stalk something around the bend on the path ahead. Taabe looked up from the dead wolf, sniffed the air, and followed her. Now, my curiosity was worked up considerably. It never ceased to amaze me how animals communicated—if only we'd listen. I followed Taabe and Mua with Paint behind me. Rounding the bend, I was startled to see a dead and partially devoured Indian. I had no idea what tribe the victim might have been from, but a big cat had been at him. His bow and quiver of arrows lay nearby. The arrows matched the shaft that had killed the wolf. I carefully surveilled the scene. There were several wolf footprints, perhaps made by as many as a half dozen. Then, there were the paw prints of the mountain lion. I worked at piecing the scene together from the evidence at hand. I surmised that the Indian had been defending against the wolfpack and shot one. The hungry lion appeared and wasted no time attacking him. The wolves, having lost what may have been their pack leader, retreated in the face of the big cat. It wasn't a common scenario on the frontier, but not an unlikely one.

Taabe and Mua remained distressed. My eyes searched the surrounding area. Was the mountain lion still around and waiting for us to leave his prey?

Paint began to prance about, taking a defensive stance with ears erect and nostrils flared. Taabe and Mua both looked off to my left at a rock outcropping. I slowly looked up. Looking back at me was a penetrating set of yellow eyes and a tan critter with a long, twitching tail. A hiss and baring of fangs followed the eye contact. The hunter was looking to finish his dinner, and we stood in his way. Was it to be fight or flight? I could easily have drawn my Colt and put a bullet into the big cat's face. Would that have been just? No. I began to back away, being sure to extend my distance from the dead Indian. I didn't want to appear to threaten the mountain lion in his obvious desire to finish his meal. "Taabe," I whispered. Reluctantly yet amazingly, he backed away beside me and followed by Mua. Paint needed no encouragement. He'd have bolted were it not for me. Soon, we put enough distance from the lion that he left his perch and headed for his dinner. He kept his eyes on us the entire time, even as he took his first bites. We couldn't get out of his sight fast enough.

I wasn't sure what sort of effect the dead wolf might have on Taabe and Mua. It wasn't until nightfall, as we camped, that he took his usual place lying beside me as I lay in my bedroll. Taabe would eventually lead a pack of his own. He would learn to be a leader, the one who sets the direction of the pack. He would be loyal and display courage, exercise discipline, ensure teamwork and social order, and be the dominant nurturer of members of the pack. He would display the characteristics humans sought in great leaders. Thus, it was little wonder that Comanche, Lakota, and other nations venerated the wolf. That Taabe was with me communicated to others that I was part of his pack.

CHAPTER 11

CROW WAR PARTY

We were about four days from our destination, when I pulled up sharply on Paint's reins. Perhaps a bit more than a quarter mile off was a large band of Indians on horseback. So far as I could make out, and having so recently been in the company of Crow scouts, they appeared to be of that tribe. Shadows were lengthening in the late afternoon light. It would be ever more difficult to see clearly. There were at least four captives that I could make out, two children and two women. The captives were on long rawhide tethers and on foot, staggering along in the dust of the ponies. Whenever they fell, they'd be yanked roughly to their feet. I had no idea what tribe the captives might have been from, though I had heard that the Crow were constantly fighting with the Lakota. If they were from Crazy Horse's people, the chief wouldn't rest until they were recovered. My guess was that they had attacked the Oglala Lakota encampment while Crazy Horse was busy watching the Yellowstone Expedition. I reckoned it would be wise to keep my distance.

The band was headed in the same direction as I was. Their path had just happened to intersect with mine. While I dearly yearned to be back at the Circled Cross Ranch sooner rather than later, my innate curiosity compelled me to follow the war party. Perhaps it was a tug from my vision quest. If the captives were Oglala Lakota, maybe I could help. I patted Paint's neck. "We're going to slow down," I told him as though he fully comprehended.

With the captives on foot, I figured the Crow couldn't be traveling very far. They must have an encampment within a day's journey. Taabe sensed that something was afoot, as he was especially alert. After the meeting with Buffalo Man and the brush with the mountain lion, he seemed ready for more excitement. It remained to be seen as to whether he matched the bravery of his alpha male sire, Zeb.

* * *

How close to the war party could I get? I wanted to get a closer look at the captives, not that I expected to know them. Still, it would personalize this adventure for me. While it was likely my Comanche breeding, it gave me a sense of purpose. I was looking for life purpose, and this might be a first step if indeed I could help the captives.

I looked far off to the east as a hint of campfire smoke drifted into the sky. It was enough that I suspected that it was the Crow encampment. I also observed some greater activity among the warriors and what looked to be shouting, though, being upwind, I was unable to hear. I decided to venture closer. A line of lodgepole pine with a sprinkling of quaking aspen dotted the hillside above the strung-out war party column. I was of a mind to wend my way to those trees and use them as cover while positioning close enough to the Crow to better see the prisoners. The Crow were paying no attention to their back trail, as they were confident that Crazy Horse was still involved up on the Yellowstone River. Thus, I easily crossed behind them and made my way among the trees. Paint sensed the stealth of our task and neither whinnied nor snorted despite climbing the surprisingly steep hillside featuring those all-important trees.

We were now about fifty yards from the Crow. I dismounted and moved in parallel with their still strung-out column. Now, I was able to get a pretty much unobstructed view of the prisoners. The children were boys and doing their best to remain as stoic as they could in the face of so fearsome an enemy. They couldn't have been older than nine or ten years. The first of the captive women I saw was not much older than the boys. The second woman walked with her head held high despite her circumstances. She was covered in trail dust. A Crow warrior shouted at her, and she made the motions of spitting in his direction, though her mouth was bone dry. Suddenly, I recognized her. She was my beautiful Morning Star! I now found myself filled with a great sense of purpose. The Crow would not have her!

What might I possibly do between where we were and the Crow encampment? Given the distance of the smoke and the time of day, there was a good chance that they might camp. With the North Platte close by, there was plentiful water. Then again, would they push on into the night?

The warriors halted. Those who appeared to be the leaders gathered together, likely to discuss whether to push on. One pointed to the captives as though pleading that they couldn't go on much longer. Others pointed eastward toward the distant spot from which I'd seen smoke.

Much to my surprise, the Crow divided their band. Most headed back on the trail, while what looked to be not more than ten warriors began making camp. The captives were brought together and tied as securely as possible to an aspen a mere twenty yards from where I hid with Paint and the wolves. It was a blessing that they were so careless. They made a fire and gathered round, talking animatedly about what I guessed had been the attack on the Lakota encampment. They laughed and carried on so, that I wondered whether they'd ever get to sleep. I hoped to have a chance to rescue the captives, especially Morning Star. Defeating ten seasoned warriors was a tall order, but being young and a bit fool-hardy compensated for good sense. I hoped Taabe and Mua would help.

The foolish Crow failed to post even one sentry. They hobbled their ponies in a loose-knit remuda not far from the tree they tied the Lakota prisoners to. The warriors laughed and carried on such that I thought they might never go to sleep.

I observed the two young boys. They were dead tired and quickly fell asleep. The younger of the two women lay back and closed her eyes, while Morning Star looked about as though seeking a way to escape.

The Crow had just about fallen asleep, and I prepared to make my move, when one of the warriors got up to answer nature's call. He walked outside the camp circle to within a mere body length of me. My Bowie knife was already unsheathed. As the Crow squatted, I stepped behind and slashed his throat. He never made but a gurgling sound as he toppled dead in the dirt. One down.

I tried to get Morning Star's attention. The remaining nine Crow were sleeping, but any sudden noise could spell trouble.

Taabe strode around the campsite and stood about ten feet from Morning Star. She began to scream but choked it back, as Taabe cocked his head like a common dog. He walked back to me, and that was when she saw me. I put my finger to my lips to ensure her silence. I wondered what my chances were of killing nine sleeping Crow warriors one by one without raising any alarm? Yet, I had to improve the odds.

I snuck around to where Morning Star and the others were tied. The grateful expression on her face made my heart skip a beat. Better, her eyes revealed that she recognized me. There was no time for niceties. I had to focus on the delicate work ahead. I cut her loose while she nearly melted me with her eyes, then handed her the knife to free the other woman while I covered the mouths of the two boys with my hands to keep them silent. Once freed, the other woman helped keep the boys calm and quiet as Morning Star and I headed for the Crow remuda. I made an owl call. Paint's ears perked up, and he quietly joined us. My plan was to mount the captives on the Crow ponies and stampede those remaining while we made our getaway.

I had gotten the women and boys mounted and was about to chase off the other ponies, when a Crow awakened. I slapped the rumps of the horses, sending the captives galloping away while I leaped into Paint's saddle and tried to stampede the ponies while freeing my Spencer carbine. The Crow grabbed my leg with an iron grip. He was unarmed, but the other warriors began to awaken. I dealt the warrior a crushing blow to the face with the butt of my rifle and dug my heels into Paint's sides. We were off as though shot from a cannon. We charged through the cluster of warriors who were just beginning to nock arrows toward stopping my escape. I hugged Paint as we galloped recklessly ahead and soon caught up with the now freed Lakota.

We galloped on for about two miles before I grabbed the halter on Morning Star's mount band brought us to a halt. We were all breathless. In the moonlight, I saw great relief on their faces. We dared not tarry long. The Crow would surely recover some of their ponies and be after us. They could never face the embarrassment of losing their prisoners. I reckoned there were only eight fight-worthy warriors left and that they'd likely recover no more than four of the six stampeded ponies. That would be four too many for my liking.

"We must keep going," I signed, and spoke in English.

Morning Star smiled and nodded.

I paused and looked at her. Her dress was tattered. She was covered with trail dust and bore scratches and bruises from the attack, yet she was beautiful to my eyes.

She shifted as though in discomfort and shook her head. "Awentia *wiiyukta* Wiiyophan Kin," she said, with a tone of regret. She pointed in the direction of the Lakota encampment and urged her pony forward.

Paint and I stood unmoving. What was she telling me? Who or what was Wiiyophan Kin? I found myself torn between heading to the Freemans' ranch and following Morning Star to be sure she reached home safely. Behind me in the direction of the ranch, I was sure to meet a small band of embarrassed Crow warriors. Ahead of me were the Lakota with whom I was sort of friends, and of course, Morning Star.

* * *

I quickly caught up with the freed captives. We maintained as fast a pace as the ponies could endure. I kept an eye on our backtrail, peeling off every now and then to see whether we were followed. Taabe and Mua followed along, though I was convinced Mua might have pups any day. I didn't mind positioning at the rear of our little party, as I could keep Morning Star in my sights. I still found myself trying to figure what she had told me. The image of her coming to care for me months back in that Oglala Lakota teepee stuck in my mind. She was so sweet and caring. What had happened since? Then, it hit me. She was fourteen and of age for marriage. She was promised to a Lakota warrior.

I felt as though someone had thrown a bucket of cold water over me. Was the love of my life not to be mine? Who was Wiiyophan Kin?

The ponies were tiring. "Awentia!" I called.

She slowed and twisted to look back at me.

I pointed to the horses and then to a stand of quaking aspen.

She understood and turned her pony toward the trees.

We all dismounted. A quick search revealed a small stream, so we watered our mounts and slaked our own thirsts.

Morning Star and the other girl washed much of the trail dust from their faces and arms. Had the water been deeper, it wouldn't have surprised me if they'd jumped in for a bath.

As I let Paint drink his fill, I found myself staring at Morning Star, mesmerized. She was very much the Morning Star that her name translated to. But she was the Morning Star of another.

She caught me staring, and a winsome smile betrayed

her feelings for me. Perhaps, she had no feelings for this Wiiyophan Kin warrior. It could be an arrangement made by her father, as was often the case among the tribes. She pointed westward. "Tasunke Witko," she said, and made signs for a village. Then her face went sad, as she apparently thought on the attack that led to her capture by the Crow.

CHAPTER 12

AWENTIA

With ponies rested, we mounted up. There was still no sign of pursuing Crow. They may have gone for reinforcements, figuring to assault the Lakota encampment again and seek their revenge. They knew that a lone White man in buckskins and riding a Pinto pony had shamed them. I felt sure they'd like little better than to capture me.

We had ridden a couple of more miles when I saw a dust cloud little more than a half mile off and approaching from the northeast. It wasn't quite the direction I expected the Crow to emerge from. "Awentia!" I called out. Catching her attention, I pointed toward the approaching dust.

She immediately turned her pony into a stand of aspen. We all followed to hide among the trees until we could identify the riders bearing down upon us.

As they grew closer, it became obvious that they were Indians.

Morning Star let out a yelp, and she pressed her heels

hard into her pony's flanks. "Tathanka! *Ate*! *Ate*!" she shouted as she sprang from the trees.

My friend Tatkanka had caught up to us. He pulled up upon seeing Morning Star galloping toward them.

I led the remaining Lakota from the trees. As I approached the reunion, Morning Star was hugging a Lakota warrior and babbling excitedly about what had happened and how I had rescued them. I had no idea who she was hugging, but he appeared old enough to be her father rather than a young warrior to whom she was betrothed.

Buffalo Man smiled at me with gratitude. He held up ten fingers to represent the ten Crow warriors Morning Star had described.

The warrior Morning Star had been hugging, broke free and rode over to me. He pointed to himself. "Wapi-tiyu Okle," he said, then pointed to Morning Star and back to himself. "*Ate*," he said, and brought his hands together in a sign for family.

Now, I understood. This was her father. I'd later learn that his name translated to Spotted Elk. I was about to respond when my eyes caught a dozen Crow warriors riding hard out of the east.

Buffalo Man saw them as well. "*Kize*! *Katá*!" he shouted and waved his rifle aloft. The Lakota wasted no time. Riding far fresher ponies, Tatkanka led the charge at the Crow, who were taken by surprise. Instead of a man with harmless young captives, they'd run into an angry Lakota war party. Morning Star had told of the attack on the village and the killing of many innocent women and children while Crazy Horse was away.

The Lakota and Crow merged in battle with yelps and whoops, rifle fire, and lances spearing. The quarters were too close for bows and arrows, but knives and clubs were in play. A Crow warrior broke free of the battle and headed for me.

I calmly raised my Spencer carbine and took careful aim. As I was about to pull the trigger, an image flashed by in my peripheral vision.

Wielding a tree branch as a club, Morning Star was charging at the Crow.

I took my finger from the trigger for fear of hitting her.

She caught the savage by surprise. She swung her makeshift club with such force that the Crow was unhorsed. He fell unceremoniously into a cluster of prickly pear cactus. In addition to his pride, his backside was in pain. Morning Star sprang from her pony like a cat and was on the helpless warrior with her club. Two hefty wallops and the warrior breathed his last.

I glanced out to where the battle was winding down. The Lakota were clearly winning. I dismounted and walked to Morning Star.

She was standing breathlessly over the dead warrior. Upon realizing that I was beside her, she dropped her club and embraced me tightly. I felt her sobs in my chest. "Isa...Isa," she murmured. She remembered my name. I was in momentary heaven as she pressed against me. It was as though she was releasing an avalanche of pent-up emotions. However, our tryst was not to last.

Buffalo Man rode up along with Wapitiyu Okle and five surviving Lakota warriors. The Crow had been wiped out. Bloody scalps abounded.

Wapitiyu Okle looked at Morning Star as she gently pushed away from me. "Wiiyophan Kin," he said with an admonishing tone.

For me, it was an ill-timed reminder of her being promised to another.

Buffalo Man looked at me and then at the dead Crow warrior and the tree branch on the ground beside Morning Star. He locked eyes with her. *"Katá?"* he asked roughly.

Morning Star nodded.

Buffalo Man made a cutting motion across his hairline and handed his knife to her.

I had learned that it was not uncommon for women to take scalps, but never witnessed it.

Morning Star looked at Buffalo Man, then her father, and finally at me. She took a deep breath, bent over the dead savage, and deftly took his scalp.

To say that the act cast her in a new light for me would be putting it mildly. Here I was, a half-White teen raised in a Christian household with strong Bible-based values, facing a bewildering set of emotions over a Lakota girl who had captured my heart.

She raised her hand high, displaying the scalp, blood running down her arm. The warriors shouted approval.

"Isa," said Buffalo Man. He pointed in the direction of the Oglala Lakota encampment.

I nodded. Of course, I'd join in both the mourning and celebration. Such was life on the frontier. As I mounted Paint, I caught the emotionally torn look in Morning Star's eyes. By virtue of my happening upon her and her captors by pure chance, my Morning Star had been thrust into the emotional and cultural entanglement between her betrothal to another and her love for me.

* * *

As we rode toward the Lakota encampment, Tatkanka explained that Morning Star's grandfather was Lone

Horn, a chief of the Miniconjou Lakota. Her betrothal was apparently of a somewhat political nature, designed to bring the two Lakota subtribes together. Apparently, relations between the Oglala and Miniconjou were strained. Having heard about Sitting Bull's Hunkpapa Lakota, I sensed that something big was brewing.

Buffalo Man gave me a sympathetic look. As battle-tested a warrior as he was, he must have noticed the flirtations between Morning Star and me. "*WiiyA*," he said with a sign for danger added for emphasis. "Tatanka Wiiyaska *nanpí!*"

So, the warrior Morning Star was promised to, was named Buffalo Killer, and he was of a jealous nature. From Buffalo Man's gestures, he was no one to mess with. The Lakota didn't take kindly to folks interfering in betrothals and especially marriages. Even the mighty Crazy Horse had suffered for having an adulterous affair.

The encampment was still cleaning up from the Crow attack as we headed toward Crazy Horse's teepee. The dead had been buried, and the mourning process was still ongoing. Several teepees had been burned and a couple badly torn. The wounded were being treated by the shaman. Nearly all of the victims had been women, children, and the elderly.

"Crow *wiiyuka*," intoned Buffalo Man as we rode deeper into the encampment.

From his tone, I assumed he'd called the Crow cowards. Attacking weak foes was certainly a cowardly act. Beating the Crow earlier in the day was clearly insufficient. There would surely be a near-future attack on the Crow. I assumed they would not plan any attack until Crazy Horse returned.

Morning Star was greeted as a heroine for having

vanquished the Crow warrior. Her humility and even shyness at the adulation was endearing to me. Despite being surrounded by Lakota women, she managed to smile at me. Having killed and taken a scalp in battle, I wondered whether she could return to the womanly chores of camp life. Would she follow the Lakota way?

Buffalo Man directed me to a teepee that had apparently belonged to an elderly couple killed in the Crow attack. Normally, it would have been destroyed, but this situation was not normal. He signed that they would eat soon and to join him and his wife.

I gave Paint his freedom and settled into the teepee for some much-needed rest. I still wanted to get to the Freeman spread, but I felt that there was unfinished business here. The Oglala Lakota had endured the pain of a cowardly attack, and their pain needed to be assuaged. Perhaps, it was the Comanche in me that empathized, but it was just as likely the magnetic pull of Morning Star. Pa had shared the writings of a man named Shakespeare, who wrote about Romeo and Juliet. They were called star-crossed lovers, because the obstacles to their love were too great. I prayed that I'd be no star-crossed lover with Morning Star. Did I say *love*? Were these attractions to this young Lakota girl what love was? Yet, she was promised to Tatanka Wiiyaska. I thought back to the story Pa and Ma told of their courtship. She was daughter to the great Penateka Comanche Chief Buffalo Hump and the sister to my pa's friend Spirit Talker. She had pursued Pa and even killed a Comanche shaman to save his life.

That I'd seen Morning Star unclothed when she treated my wounds did linger in my mind, try as I might to wash he image away in keeping with the Christian morals taught to me. I apologized to God, as it was forever imprinted in my consciousness.

It occurred to me that I'd not seen Taabe in several hours. He and Mua had followed me to the edge of the encampment, then I lost track. It wasn't unusual for them to disappear occasionally, but I was curious, given Mua's condition.

* * *

I enjoyed a meal with Buffalo Man. Afterward, I decided to return to the teepee and catch some sleep. I was just about asleep when Taabe appeared. He acted as though he wanted me to follow him, so I obliged. Dusk was settling on the encampment as he led me deep into the forest. We'd gone a couple of miles when he stopped and sniffed the air. He gave an uncharacteristic yip. His call was returned, and we proceeded to a cave-like overhang which housed Mua and five wolf pups. If a wolf can make the facial expression of a proud papa, Taabe did his best to pull it off. He went over and licked Mua and nuzzled the pups. He gazed up at me invitingly, so I walked over and was soon fondling the litter of little creatures. Taabe was building his pack. There appeared to be three females and two males, and every one was an energetic ball of fur scrambling over each other to get to their mother's teat.

I spent better than an hour with Taabe's brood and headed back to the teepee. I encountered one sentry, but he quickly recognized me, and I passed on with no problem. He did say that Crazy Horse was expected the next day.

Images of Taabe, Mua, and the pups lingered in my

mind, as I grew drowsy and began to fall asleep. Just as sleep overtook me, the teepee flap swished open.

Morning Star stepped in with a panicked look on her face. "Tatanka Wiiyaska come tomorrow," she said in broken English. "We go now!" she declared.

The last thing I needed was to have an angry warrior and unsympathetic Lakota chasing me over a woman. Oh, how I burned to run away with Morning Star. I stood and embraced her trembling body. "Awentia *winyan* Tatanka Wiiyaska," I reminded her. She was to be Buffalo Killer's woman.

She pulled back. Tears streamed down her cheeks. Morning Star pointed to herself. "Isa *winyan*," she stated firmly, as though it was not to be questioned.

"Isa talk with Tasunke Witko," I promised her. Perhaps, the chief could resolve this dilemma of true love versus politics.

"Isa *winyan*," she repeated. She caressed my cheek and left me standing there in the middle of the teepee. How was I to sleep? How was I to handle Tatanka Wiiyaska? The warrior's name was fearsome enough. Buffalo Killer! It takes a strong warrior to kill a buffalo.

* * *

Crazy Horse rode at the head of the column of Oglala Lakota. They had enjoyed a measure of success against the expedition on the Yellowstone River in their battle with Custer's Seventh Cavalry. They held their proud heads high.

The mighty chief had been alerted in advance of the Crow attack. He was none too pleased at the aftermath. Despite efforts to bring order to the encampment, evidence yet abounded. He saw me and gave a grateful nod. He'd apparently been told of my efforts to rescue Morning Star and the others from the clutches of the Crow. However, his people were still in mourning. This demanded his attention.

I stayed close to my borrowed teepee, awaiting the opportunity to meet with Crazy Horse. I felt that I was forging a détente with the Lakota.

As the sun dipped below the horizon, I was summoned to the teepee of the chief. As I emerged from my teepee, I scanned the encampment for Taabe and Mua. They had not reappeared. Taabe was taking his family responsibility to heart and steering clear of human company.

I entered the teepee of Crazy Horse. "Greetings, Tasunke Witko," I said. The stern look on his face set me aback.

"Isa must go," he said. "Leave Lakota."

Behind him stood my Morning Star with a fierce-looking warrior who must have been Buffalo Killer. He stood with fire in his eyes. From what I could gather, Morning Star's feelings for me must have been discussed, but the commitment to Buffalo Killer had won the day. I was likely fortunate to be told to leave without having to fight her betrothed. To say it was an unwelcome shock would put it mildly. I dared not exchange even a brief glance with Morning Star for fear of inciting Buffalo Killer's wrath.

Crazy Horse nodded for me to leave.

I looked directly at Buffalo Killer. "Tatanka Wiiyaska peace," I said and exited. I dearly wanted to behold Morning Star one more time, but knew better. Crazy Horse had offered me a way out. I respected him and treasured my friendship with the Lakota greatly. It wouldn't do any good to destroy that, even over so lovely a woman as Morning Star. I gathered my belongings and headed for Paint. There was no point in staying and tempting fate. I could make several miles toward the ranch under the moonlit night.

I climbed aboard Paint and turned him to head eastward. Out of my peripheral vision, I caught a glimpse of Morning Star. I dared not look but hunkered down and left the encampment. I thanked the Lord that I had the character to not turn us into a Romeo and Juliet.

Recalling the location of the Crow encampment, I swung well south. It wouldn't be long before they felt the wrath of Crazy Horse's Lakota warriors. Don't get me wrong, Texas is beautiful and possesses scenic marvels that I love, but there's a majesty to much of the country I was now traversing. The rocky peaks, primeval forests, crystalline rivers, and rushing waterfalls of central Wyoming were awe-inspiring. Shucks, I'd just come from tracing the Yellowstone River and all its beauty.

Try as I might to think on my surroundings, I was unable to get Morning Star out of my mind. Should I have challenged Buffalo Killer? What would God have me do?

CHAPTER 13

BREED

By my reckoning, I was a mere two days from the Circled Cross Ranch. I was rather proud of myself that I'd found my way despite hair-raising distractions, and of course, Morning Star. Each morning, I'd awaken to clear skies and—you guessed it—a *morning star* hanging in the pre-sunrise sky. Did God tease us mortals? Seems like.

Paint was sure-footing it on a narrow rocky. As we rounded a bend, two riders blocked our way. There was no room to pass, but they didn't look like passing was on their minds. They were nasty-looking. Scraggly beards and bloodshot eyes peeked from under broad-brimmed hats. They wore buckskins common to the region and carried old muzzle-loading flintlocks. One of them was already aimed at me. I began to back Paint to a place where passing was feasible.

"Yuh stop right thar, pard," said the larger of the two. He might have had two teeth in his mouth and a deep scar ran from chin to ear. "We be wantin' thet thar hoss of yurs."

"I don't think that'd be a good idea," I replied.

"You be a breed ain't yuh," said the second man. "Yuh breeds be a bunch of cowards," he added and spat tobacco a slug of juice.

The first man cocked the hammer of his flintlock.

Now, these two were about twenty feet away, and I was staring down the muzzle of an old but likely service-able musket. I had no time to reach for my Spencer, and being seated in the saddle made drawing my Colt challenging at best.

"Stop messin' 'round, Chuck. Just kill him. He be a no-good breed anyhow."

Chuck smiled as he pulled the trigger. I saw a flash, but nothing happened.

"Dang, Chuck! Yuh din't load her!" exclaimed Chuck's companion.

With that, Chuck grabbed the musket's forestock, urged his horse forward, and began swinging the gun like a club. "Yer a dead man, breed!" he hollered.

I didn't take especially kindly to being called a breed but less kindly to being attacked. Chuck was closing fast. He was so close that I smelled the heavy scent of liquor on his breath. My Bowie knife flashed in the morning sun. As I ducked under the arc of his swinging musket, I brought the knife up into his stomach just beneath his rib cage. It was an ugly feeling as his weight forced the knife to its hilt. The knife is a very personal weapon. Pa told me about how soldiers in the War Between the States were often never the same after bayoneting an enemy. Indians with their lances and war clubs were all-too-familiar with the personal, close-in nature of many battles.

Chuck's eyes opened wide as he immediately realized

he'd been killed. My knife had split his gut open and cut straight up into his heart. The inertia from his musket, combined with his heavy body, caused him to fall away from me. Still in the saddle, man and his horse plummeted down the steep drop-off from the trail. I watched for but a second before turning my attention to Chuck's companion. Raising the knife in my blood-soaked hand, I waved it threateningly at him. He desperately tried to turn his horse, but the beast lost its footing. He tumbled over the trail edge, joining his friend in a heap at the bottom. Did I hear him say that breeds were cowards?

I stared at my bloody hand. What had I done? Two men were dead, and I sat there on Paint with my knife and the silence of the mountainside. I dismounted and poured water from my bota bag over my hand and knife. I heard a faint whinny from the jumble of men and horses.

Staring over the trail's edge, I saw the panicky look in the eyes of one horse with a badly broken leg. I took out my Spencer rifle and put the poor beast out of its misery. The boom of the rifle and its echo brought the silence of the forested trail into greater contrast.

The trail ahead was clear. Sadly, there was nothing I could do about the dead men and horses in the ravine. The drop-off was steep and had no easy approach. It was far too rocky to hope to bury the men, so I prayed to my Lord that he'd forgive me for leaving them to the creatures of the wilderness.

Who were they? What had brought them to that place before me? Why had they challenged me? I'd never know. I took a final look at the litter below and urged Paint on.

I dwelled for a moment on that term the men had

called me: *breed*. A couple of troopers in Colonel Stanley's expedition called me by that epithet. In my experience thus far, it seemed that only Whites used it, and it was of a derogatory nature. I sensed it wouldn't be my first or last confrontation with prejudice.

The trail played out and opened onto a vista as carved by the North Platte River. Another day, and I'd be riding into George's ranch.

I caught sight of the Oregon Trail far off in the distance. I likely wouldn't have noticed it yet, but for the sunlight reflecting off the white canvas of a caravan of prairie schooners bringing the next wave of settlers to the West Coast. I turned Paint toward them. They'd undoubtedly passed by George's ranch, so it seemed logical that they might have some news.

* * *

I found myself approaching the wagon train from the west. They seemed especially slow-moving. Their travels would be getting markedly slower as they moved into the mountains. The man riding point looked to be well-outfitted, a little dandyish, but well-outfitted. He held his head high, and even his horse seemed to exhibit an attitude.

From my vantage point, it looked as though several of the wagons were out of sorts. That is, there had been some hasty sewing repairs made to tears in their bonnets, and some had half their bonnets missing. One wagon was partially burned. They'd obviously been in a fight, but looked to have come out of it mostly intact.

As I drew closer, I hollered in perfectly good English, "Hail the train!" Maybe it was my sitting on a Pinto pony with my long braided dark hair, combined with the buckskins and the bow and arrows, but the point man pulled out his rifle and fired a shot just over my head. I ducked in my saddle and pulled Paint to a halt.

"Indians!" he hollered, motioning for men from the wagon train to join him.

I pulled up. "Peace!" I yelled at the top of my lungs.

Three men on horseback joined this fellow, who was apparently the wagon master. He pointed my way, raised his rifle again, and fired. I was grateful that he had terrible marksmanship. Then, the others opened fire.

I knew when I wasn't wanted. I pivoted Paint and broke at a gallop for the hills to my left. The wagon master and the others headed my way for perhaps a quarter mile before calling off the chase.

Breathing hard and curious as to why they reacted as they did, I nevertheless wasn't going to hang around for answers. Life sure had taken an interesting turn. Where was my vision quest leading me? What was God's plan? I'd been forced to leave the Lakota, had encountered the two ne'er-do-wells on the trail, and now was chased off by a wagon master with a bad attitude against anyone resembling an Indian.

I'd have one more night of camping before reaching the ranch. I rode well beyond the end of the wagon train, staying hidden in the tree line. I looked forward to asking George about them. They may have had an experience that soured them on the Red man.

With the wagon train out of sight, I returned to the Oregon Trail. I hadn't gone but a couple of miles when I came upon why the men behaved as they had. There were five fresh graves and a partially burned wagon lying on its side. There was some litter from the burned wagon, mostly clothing and pieces of furniture. I reckoned folks had retrieved whatever they felt was salvageable. It saddened me to confront this sad reality of folks moving westward.

* * *

I had arrived in more familiar country. The rushing crystalline waters of the North Platte had become like a dear friend. Early in my visit with the Freemans, I'd explored it and its tributaries. It offered rewarding fishing spots, and importantly, great shelters for camping. I could build a fire that wasn't likely to be detected except by the most experienced woodsman.

I had the good fortune to spot a rabbit that fell victim to one of my arrows. A little fresh meat for dinner was in order. I enjoyed roast rabbit and the last of my coffee, along with a few berries. I likely didn't need to, but I tied Paint on a long tether. He'd alert me to any danger. With any luck, I'd enjoy a peaceful night under a starlit sky. Looking up, I could almost hear the stars twinkling.

I curled up in my bedroll and soon fell asleep.

Sometime during the middle of the night, I felt something snuggle against my backside. It was reminiscent of Taabe, so I didn't stir. I had visions of waking up to those blue timber wolf eyes.

* * *

A shaft of sunlight hit my face. I'd overslept. I still felt what I figured to be Taabe nestled close in behind me. I turned ever-so-slowly. "Awentia!" I gasped.

Morning Star opened her eyes and blinked at me with a soft smile.

A mix of contradictory emotions tore through my mind. Here beside me lay the love of my life. The woman whose beauty outshone acres of Texas bluebonnets, so sweet that she made sugar seem bitter, yet courageous and frontier tough. Now, she was here with me. She'd braved the wilds of Wyoming alone to follow my trail.

I shook my head to clear my heavenly musings and face the reality at hand. I looked searchingly into her eyes. She remained betrothed to another. What of Buffalo Killer? Tracking Morning Star would be easy for him, and they'd surely waste no time assembling a dozen Lakota warriors to do just that. All this was surely happening, as I lay here with her breath mingling with mine. I bent in and kissed her. Me, who barely knew what a kiss was, had just sealed my fate with this beautiful woman. Still savoring the kiss, I pulled back gently. "Tatanka Wiiyaska?" I asked with a whisper, yearning for a God-inspired answer.

Morning Star sat bolt upright. She slammed her fist into the palm of her other hand. There'd been some sort of fight. She saw a stick, grabbed it, and broke it in two. "Tatanka Wiiyaska *zuzeca.*" She made a sign like a slithering snake. "*Winyan.*"

I knew that was the Lakota word for woman. From what she was saying, Buffalo Killer had broken their betrothal by having an affair with another woman. He was now lower than a snake, and she'd been freed of her promise to him. To my mind, and as yet inexperienced in affairs of the heart as well as the Lakota, I wasn't so sure that Buffalo Killer would have taken this well. "No Tatanka Wiiyaska?" I asked, seeking her assurance.

Morning Star repeated her words and signing, then threw up her hands as though all was well. She pulled me down to her and looked ever-so-deeply into my eyes.

We kissed, and I felt as though my lips had melted

into hers. If this was love, praise God. "How find me?" I asked mostly with signing.

She likely knew enough of the Wyoming hills and rudiments of tracking, though there was more. Morning Star pointed to the tree where Paint was tethered.

There sat Taabe and Mua with their pups. They headed to me to enjoy a great reunion.

Everything seemed to be coming together for me. Pa told us that life was a faith journey by which we grow and that God worked for our good, not necessarily our comfort. Yet, deep within me, I sensed that there would be more. I had not come upon my mission, my life purpose. Morning Star began rustling up some coffee and found the last of my jerky. I'd begun to think of her in the English translation of her name rather than Awentia. Would the same logic work for me? Somehow, Isa tripped on the tongue for me better than Wolf, plus Isa was my given name.

I picked up the cup of coffee Morning Star had poured for me. Next, I looked up, and she was bathing in the North Platte. I averted my eyes, but what little I'd seen would never leave my mind. I was grateful that we were less than a day from the ranch. I'm not certain that I'd be able to contain myself beyond that. Pa and Ma had drummed the honor of marriage into our heads, and I wasn't about to defy the teachings of God and parents.

As Morning Star climbed from the river, she gave me a curious look. "*WiiyA?*" she asked tentatively.

Did she please me? Oh my, did she ever. "*WiiyA,*" I nodded.

Praise the Lord, she got dressed.

"*Sunkawaka?*" I asked. Did she have a horse?

She shook her head. "No *sunkawaka*." She had walked and run from Crazy Horse's encampment.

I'd seen her in battle and now saw her strength of love and resolve that led her to me on foot. I offered her the last of the jerky, which she reluctantly took. I walked over and patted Paint's neck. "You'll be carrying two from here on, big fella," I said soothingly. He dipped his head and seemed to understand.

* * *

We made for quite a caravan as we followed the wagon ruts of the Oregon Trail eastward. I reckoned that we'd reach George's spread by mid-afternoon. Morning Star rode behind my saddle, her arms wrapped around me. Paint patiently handled her petite body. I'd have seated her in front of me, but that was far too tempting an arrangement. I reckoned God wouldn't be approving of what danced through my mind. Chastity and patience had become a considerable challenge for me.

By my observations, we'd reach the ranch by mid-afternoon. Yet lingering in my mind was whether Buffalo Killer would pursue Morning Star and me. I prayed that Buffalo Man and Crazy Horse would have cooled the warrior's ardor. The trail ahead appeared clear, but I remained cautious.

The trail was easy to follow thanks to the wagon ruts and the litter of past travelers. With the mountains looming ahead on their westward journey, settlers jettisoned heavy baggage that would be excessively burdensome. I'm sure there were plenty of stories the trailside litter could tell. All was going well until we eased up over a rise in the trail, and my fears came to life. There between the wagon wheel ruts, Buffalo Killer sat astride his war pony. He was fully decked out for exacting his vengeance, and the angry eyes peering from between broad red and black stripes of warpaint fully revealed those intentions. He wore a headdress with no less than two dozen eagle feathers. It was more for show than battle, yet impressive nonetheless. He was bare-chested but for a bone breastplate, and he wore beaded buckskin leggings and moccasins. Scalps dangled from his lance, and a war club hung on a thong from his waist. His pony —surely his best—bore plenty of painted symbols of Buffalo Killer's prowess.

"Tatanka Wiiyaska no *kize*," I said, in a commanding tone. I was a good four or five inches taller than he and a few pounds heavier. Given that and my youth, I reckoned to have an edge in hand-to-hand combat but wasn't especially anxious to engage. My only other advantage might be that the sun was behind me and shone into Buffalo Killer's eyes.

"*Kize* Awentia!" he declared with his war lance raised high. "*Kize* Isa!" It was his intention to kill us both.

My eyes swept the area. So far as I could tell, Buffalo Killer was alone. I urged Morning Star to dismount.

As she dropped to the ground, she snatched my bow and a couple of arrows. I dared not forget that this was her battle, too.

I motioned Morning Star to stay back, and she reluctantly obeyed. But she was no shrinking violet to be so easily pushed from the fray.

Buffalo Killer's eyes expressed surprise at Morning Star preparing to fight. So far as he was concerned, this was men's business first and foremost. No matter that she'd taken a Crow life and scalp in battle, she was a woman and should step away. Hatred-filled eyes glared at her. Her breaking of the betrothal and running away to me had insulted him, and made him out as less of a man.

Buffalo Killer kicked his pony's ribs hard and came galloping toward me. He aimed his lance with every intention of running me through. Even if he missed, he figured to count coup. With no bow, I pulled out my Spencer carbine as coolly as possible, levered a round into the chamber, aimed, and fired. Visions of shooting the *pistolero* months back in Texas raced through my head. My bullet hit Buffalo Killer's horse dead-on between the eyes. The pony's momentum carried it forward another couple of steps, and the war pony crumbled to its death a mere dozen feet before me. Tossed over the pony's head, Buffalo Killer lay momentarily stunned in an inglorious heap on the ground, almost underneath Big Red. With vengeance flowing hot in his veins, he revived quickly and arose with war club in hand. There was no way I could bring my carbine into play except as a club. The Lakota warrior grabbed my waistband in an attempt to pull me from Paint while bringing back his war club with the intention of delivering a death blow. Buffalo Killer's arm had just begun to arc forward, when I saw his face contort from impassioned anger to sudden pain. The war club fell harmlessly to the ground, and he grunted as his body fell against Big Red. An arrow protruded from the middle of his back. In fact, it had pierced through his body and nicked my leg.

Buffalo Killer twisted his falling body to face Morning Star. "*Kize!*" he pleaded agonizingly with blood already spewing from his lips. He begged to be killed.

I slid from my saddle and drew my Colt revolver with the intention of protecting Morning Star.

She had become every bit of the fearsome Miniconjou Lakota warrior woman that lurked within her. She set herself, nocked an arrow, drew back the bowstring, and granted Buffalo Killer's final wish. "*Kize*," she intoned.

The sheer depth of fighting passion in Morning Star's eyes caught me by surprise, though I shouldn't have been. She strode over to Buffalo Killer's dead body and took the dead warrior's knife. She was about to take his scalp.

"Awentia! No!" I declared.

She gave me a questioning look.

Amazed at her prowess, I walked over to her. "*Wowahwa*," I said in the Lakota tongue. "Peace," I translated. There had been enough passion-driven violence. It was time I began the process of sharing my faith values with the love of my life. Other than the hollow reward of vengeance, there was no good reason to desecrate the body of the fallen warrior.

Morning Star gave me a quizzical look.

"Enough. Now...*wowahwa*," I said softly but firmly. She nodded as though trying to understand.

She handed me the bow and remaining arrow, then folded herself into my arms and cried. My warrior woman had some softness in her heart. One day, we would tell our children of how their mother killed a Crow warrior in battle and later a Lakota warrior. They'd likely find themselves right committed to obeying her every command.

We stood there in each other's arms for a while. It was a mutual relief that such a threat was now removed from our lives. I could appreciate Buffalo Killer's jealous rage, but not his answer to it. Nevertheless, he was a brave warrior. I took my small shovel and dug a shallow grave while Morning Star watched. I think she was a tad perplexed, but loved me too much to protest. I wrapped Buffalo Killer in a blanket with his lance and war club and piled rocks atop the soil. Hopefully, that would discourage scavengers.

Once Buffalo Killer was buried, we resumed our journey. Morning Star wrapped her arms around my chest and leaned her head in against my back. *"Wash tay...wiiyukta,"* she said softly. I wasn't sure what that translated to, but it felt good.

CHAPTER 14

FORT LARAMIE

Running Waters was in the gallery as we headed down the lane toward the ranch house. "*Ana o'a hi'it!*" she yelled in Comanche for my benefit. Indeed, we were hungry.

Upon hearing our arrival, George came striding from the barn with a big smile pasted across his face. "Welcome home, Isa!" he declared. He froze for a moment at seeing Morning Star behind me on Paint. His smile returned bigger than ever.

I took Morning Star's hand and eased her gently to the ground before dismounting. I caught her surprised facial expression as she took in the joyous Pawnee woman holding a baby and the big, Black, smiling cowboy. She could feel their love for me.

George, Running Waters, and I, converged in the middle of the yard, with me pulling Morning Star into the cluster of love hugs. Esmeralda emerged from the house and joined in the reverie.

I had returned safe and sound. No, it was better than that. I was safe, sound, and had Morning Star. God was good. I was sure that Morning Star was part of my vision quest.

Running Waters looked at Morning Star and then at me, nodding her approval.

"George, Running Waters, meet Awentia. We reckon to marry." There, I'd said it. I hadn't even mentioned it to Morning Star, and she didn't understand my English. "*Wiiyukta, wiiyakA*," I added in Lakota.

Morning Star smiled. Love and marriage were foremost in her mind. "*Wiiyukta, wiiyakA*," she repeated with a squeeze of my hand.

"Amen!" exclaimed George. "We're going to have a wedding!" His broad, quite masculine face turned impish with the thought of it. He rubbed his hand. "Let's eat and hear of your adventures."

Hap and Dred appeared as if from nowhere with grins painted across their faces and led Paint to the barn.

* * *

It didn't take long for Running Waters and Esmeralda to fire up the oven. Morning Star began helping prepare the venison roast.

Running Waters was thrilled at her pitching in.

I was entranced by the image of the three women working together. I hadn't yet shared that my beautiful, petite Morning Star was a warrior, too.

"How was the expedition?" asked George, breaking me out of my musings.

"It was a great experience. I spent most of my time with three other scouts riding at point, so I missed much of the goings on in camp. Sergeant Rawls sort of took me under his wing. I missed a battle that Lieutenant

Colonel Custer had with Crazy Horse. I heard later that both sides claimed victory."

"What do you think of Custer?" interjected George.

I chuckled. "He seems to like himself," I responded. "He has a heart to fight the Indians, but I sense that he may one day fall to them." I don't know what inspired me to make that observation.

"They say he's a bit flamboyant," added George.

I laughed. "When the surveying was completed and Colonel Stanley began the trek back to Fort Rice, I decided to leave the expedition," I said, continuing my story. "I parted company with my fellow scouts and bade farewell to Sergeant Rawls at a place called Clark's Fork Bottom. Rawls was good enough to requisition some jerky and ammunition."

"Do you reckon to return to the Yellowstone?" asked George.

I shook my head. "Not any time soon. With winter coming on here, you'll be needing help."

"Much obliged for that, Isa. So, how did you find Awentia?" George pressed me to continue.

"I was making fairly good time on the trail. A few days in, I encountered Tathanka, whom we call Buffalo Man, the warrior who'd captured me on my journey from Texas. He had about a dozen warriors with him. I rightly figured he was with Crazy Horse, when they fought the Seventh Cavalry up with the Yellowstone Expedition. We enjoyed a meal, and he shared his expectation that Crazy Horse and a Hunkpapa Lakota chief, named Sitting Bull, were thinking of bringing the tribes together to fight the White man." I let this sink in with George. "I continued my travels. When I neared the headwaters of the North Platte, I spotted a large Crow war party with four prisoners. Two were young boys and two were young women. I watched them argue, and all but about ten warriors headed to their encampment. I figured the ten were expected to guard the prisoners. I decided to take a closer look and recognized Awentia. Her name, by the way, translates to *Morning Star*." I paused and watched the women as they prepared the meal. Morning Star had fit in easily. My, but she was so beautiful."

George brought me back from my dreaming with an incredulous laugh. "You decided to rescue her? Against ten warriors?"

I laughed. "Of course." I went on to describe how I rescued the Crow prisoners while keeping my own skin intact. "We headed toward the Oglala Lakota encampment with the embarrassed Crow warriors in pursuit. I learned that the Crow had attacked Crazy Horse's village while he was off engaging the Yellowstone Expedition. The village had been mostly defended by women, children, and the elderly. I managed to kill some Crow, but they were gaining on us, when we came upon my friend Buffalo Man. We vanquished the Crow. Awentia killed one warrior and took a scalp."

"A scalp?!" gasped George.

"She's a Lakota, George. Buffalo Man told her to take the scalp, and she obeyed." I saw that dinner was nearly ready. "We went on to Crazy Horse's encampment. Crazy Horse arrived the next day and was angered by the cowardly Crow attack. I was introduced to the warrior to whom Morning Star was promised. While the Lakota appreciated my helping rescue the four prisoners, the jealousy of her betrothed made for discomfort in the village, and I was told to leave. Sadly, I departed. I reckoned it wouldn't do to wind up like Romeo and Juliet."

George chuckled at that. "Yet, you arrived here with her."

"She escaped the Lakota village and tracked me to a place two days west of here. She told me that her betrothed, Buffalo Killer, had an affair with another woman, so the promise had been broken. I was overjoyed, but meanwhile, the jealous Buffalo Killer pursued us on his own and confronted us. He charged, and I killed his pony. Morning Star saved my life by shooting him with my bow and arrow." I paused and swallowed. "She even delivered a kill shot to relieve him of his agony. She was going to take his scalp, but I stopped her. We buried the warrior. Now, here we are."

"Morning Star is quite the warrior woman, Isa," said George, with a thoughtful scratching of his chin. "You've captured the heart of a true prize for any man of the frontier. Does she follow God?"

I smiled as the women began piling platters on the big, rough-hewn oak dining table. "We're working on that," I said to George with a wink. "We must teach her English, too."

"Sounds as though things are heating up between the Indians and our government. I don't see that fool Fort Laramie Treaty holding up. Can't say as I blame the Indians for defending themselves. Seems as though too many folks, White and Red, are willing to break promises." George sighed with resignation. "We'll do our best here," he added with determination.

"I'm sure of that," I said.

Morning Star took a seat and was about to dig in, when she realized that no one had taken a bite of food yet. She looked around and smiled quizzically at me.

"God...*Taa Naruni...Wakan Tanka*." My mind raced through translation from English to Comanche to Lakota. "*Wowahwa*," I added as it was about a blessed peace.

Morning Star nodded. When George completed the blessing, she glanced at me for approval.

I nodded with a smile and began eating.

She wasted no time.

Today, we'd begin English lessons. I even reckoned to throw in some Comanche words. With Running Waters's Pawnee tongue thrown in, there'd soon be four languages echoing around the Circled Cross Ranch. If my pa and Shorty were to drive cattle up here in the spring, Spanish would enter the language mix with the arrival of the trail cook, Perez.

* * *

Morning Star slept on a hastily made bed off in a cozy corner of the cabin, while I was relegated to the bunkhouse with Hap and Dred. That wouldn't have been so tough, but for the teasing I endured over my love for Morning Star.

They did mention that another storm baffle had been built to shelter livestock during winter storms. George sure had come up with a great solution to preserving his investment in cattle and horses.

I prayed that the ranch would survive the Indian battles that were sure to come.

"Say Isa, what'd yuh here 'bout them Injuns? There be fightin'?" asked Dred.

I had just closed my eyes to visions of Morning Star. I lifted myself to one elbow and looked over at Dred and Hap. I was speechless for a moment while shifting my thinking from love to the future of the frontier. "There'll be some small battles, Dred," I said. "But, I'm sure there'll be some big ones. The Lakota, Cheyenne, Crow...they will eventually be forced to give up their hunting grounds to the Whites."

"How kin yuh be so sure?" asked Hap.

"Mathematics," I stated flatly.

"Huh?" interjected Dred.

I chuckled. "It's just a matter of adding things up. I heard from a Lakota friend of talk in the Indian encampments, and I heard rumors among the troopers while scouting for the Yellowstone Expedition. It's mathematics, sort of. It all adds up to war."

Hap and Dred nodded in unison. "Yer purty smart fer a young'un, Isa," observed Dred.

* * *

"Isa, you up for a ride to Fort Laramie?" asked George. "I need to deliver a couple of dozen beeves."

I looked over at Morning Star. Driving cattle was generally viewed as a job performed by men. "Can Morning Star come with us?" She didn't yet understand English.

Running Waters bristled just a tad, as though saying there was woman's work to be done.

George caught her expression. "You sure about that?" He rolled his eyes out of sight of the ladies but kept his smile.

I laughed. "Morning Star would love the adventure, and I can teach her English and Comanche and open her world to God." Mostly, I didn't want to let her out of my sight.

"You think she can carry her weight?" pressed George.

"Awentia *katá* two warriors. Awentia *wasake*." I purposely threw in Lakota words, stressing that Morning Star had killed two warriors and was strong. I wanted my warrior woman to know that I spoke for her.

Running Waters rattled some pans in the washbasin and murmured something to Esmeralda. She appeared to be resigned to men doing what men decide to do. It was the way of the frontier.

"What does Morning Star want to do?" questioned George as a final challenge.

I took Morning Star's hand and I gazed into her eyes. I made signs for riding horses and herding cattle. Of course, she thought I was signing about hunting buffalo. No matter. "Do you want to come?" I asked in English while repeating the signs.

She looked at Running Waters and Esmeralda and then back at me and George. "Awentia, no *iyaya*, Isa." She signed that she didn't want to be away from me.

"You heard her. Let's get ready."

"Well, let's pick a horse for your young lady, Isa. We have some spare tack in the barn." He laughed as he headed out the door. "Dred and Hap are going to love this." He paused. "Can she handle a rifle?"

"She'll have my bow and arrows. We'll bring an extra rifle, so she can learn." I thought on that a minute. "Not to worry. No shooting around the beeves." Last thing we'd need would be a stampede.

The trip to Fort Laramie would only take a day, so we'd bring an extra horse for each drover and enough grub and supplies to carry on a mule's back.

* * *

At the crack of dawn, we began driving our small herd eastward, pretty much following the Oregon Trail. I rode drag with Morning Star with Dred and Hap at the flanks and George riding point.

I rode up beside Morning Star and pointed to a lingering star in the early morning sky. "Awentia," I said, pointing at her and then the star. "Morning Star," I added with the same motions.

She pointed to herself. "Morning Star." She smiled and gave me a look that was downright dangerous, given that we weren't married yet. "Morning Star," she repeated.

Taabe was following along, but I decided not to get into translating my name, given that I preferred Isa to Wolf.

I pointed to the beeves lumbering along before us. "Cattle," I said.

Morning Star looked from me to the longhorns. "Cattle," she repeated.

I nodded. Our English lesson had begun well.

Unfortunately, I wasn't able to ride beside Morning Star all morning, as the cattle occasionally had to be reminded that they were with other beeves. Riding drag is usually a dusty business, but a misty early rain had kept the dust to a minimum. We did stop to accommodate Morning Star answering nature's call. Given that trail drives were overwhelmingly worked by men, women's needs didn't usually need consideration.

With a small herd, we were able to cover the twenty or so miles in a single day, though it was nearly dark when Fort Laramie came into sight. George figured there was no point in hailing the fort so late in the day, so we bedded down the herd for the night. We'd take turns standing watch.

With Colonel Stanley and Lieutenant Colonel Custer still up at Fort Rice with the surveyors and better than a thousand troops, the garrison at Fort Laramie was thin. Custer was likely itching to get his Seventh Cavalry back into action. Rumor had it that General Sherman was of a mind to eradicate what was called the *Indian Problem* once and for all. It wouldn't surprise me if Custer headed out on another jaunt along the Yellowstone River. I hadn't yet figured out what to make of the man. Of course, I'd not met him directly, so it wasn't my place to make judgments based upon hearsay.

George did venture over to the fort to alert them to our presence. When he returned, we built a small fire to heat up coffee while chowing down on venison jerky. Dred took first watch. Notably, George made certain that Morning Star bedded down at what he judged to be an acceptable distance from me. George did permit us to hug before hitting our bedrolls. She took it well, though just about melted me with a lingering look of longing.

I took second shift, saddling Paint and pausing to make small talk with Dred. Dred advised me not to sing. There was apparently some grouchy old bull that didn't take kindly to melodic tones. The bull was safe, as I couldn't sing a lick anyway.

I guessed that it was just after midnight when I heard stirrings from the fort. I strained my eyes to make out what was going on. Under the moonlight, a rider rode in. He was in a hurry. I could sense the sweat and lather from a quarter mile away. I shrugged, wondering what that might be about. It'd have to wait until morning.

Morning Star stirred. I rode over beside her. "Sleep," I told her, and placed my hands together beside my head. "I'll take your watch." I pointed to myself and then to the herd.

Her dark eyes looked at me. "Morning Star sleep," she echoed.

As I turned to rejoin the herd, I saw that George had awakened. He looked at me, winked, and went back to sleep. He was making sure that Morning Star remained an honest woman.

* * *

Come dawn, we mustered ourselves to the task of driving the herd to the entrance of Fort Laramie. I must say, as a young but experienced cowhand, George was delivering prime beef. The garrison would be well fed for weeks.

As we prepared to herd them out, I rode up beside George. "Sometime after midnight, a rider rode hard into the fort. It seemed to cause quite a stir."

He nodded thoughtfully. "Happens all the time, Isa. But you never know. It could be big news."

We drove the herd the final distance to the fort.

While Dred and Hap watched the herd, George, Morning Star, and I ventured into the fort to finish our business. A couple of trooper jaws gaped a tad at the sight of a Black cowboy, a half-breed teen, and a Lakota woman walking side-by-side past them. We strode straight to headquarters.

"Is the lieutenant in?" asked George.

"Howdy, Mr. Freeman," responded a smiling corporal. "I'll check to be sure he'll see you." He turned and headed to the lieutenant's office.

George winked at Morning Star and me. "Lieutenant Richards might have had one too many last night," he whispered.

The corporal returned. "He'll see you. Go right on in," he said with an apologetic smile.

George knocked on the lieutenant's door.

"Come in, George."

Upon entering, I was nearly overcome by the strong smell of alcohol. Morning Star gave me a concerned look. She'd seen what happened to Indians over-imbibing the White man's firewater.

"Good morning, Lieutenant Richards. I'm pleased to introduce my friend Jack O'Toole's son, Isa, and his friend, Morning Star."

Richards remained seated behind his desk and wiped his runny nose with his tunic sleeve. He didn't look to be in a mood for extended conversation. To my thinking, he looked a bit old for being a junior officer. I reckoned George might fill me in later. "How many?" he said curtly but softly, as though the sound of his voice hurt his head. It likely did.

"Twenty-five all fattened up and ready for trooper stomachs, Lieutenant," responded George.

Richards nodded and scribbled a note, which he offered to George. "Give this to the quartermaster." The lieutenant then turned to me. "What tribe runs in your veins, Isa?"

Frankly, it was none of his business. "Comanche, sir," I responded respectfully.

"And the woman?" he pressed.

Morning Star read the lieutenant like sign on a trail. "Oglala Lakota," she said proudly.

"She understands English?" he asked.

George was feeling uncomfortable with the question-ing. "Will that be all, Lieutenant Richards?"

The lieutenant sat silently for a moment. "Just trying

to understand," he mumbled. His all-White world was turning upside down. He smiled patronizingly at us. "Dismissed."

Not being members of the military, I took that as an insult.

George nudged my arm, and we departed.

As we headed to the quartermaster, I turned to George. "What's his problem?"

My Black rancher friend shook his head ruefully. "Too many battles, too much liquor, and too many fights," he said with a touch of melancholy.

Morning Star saw his concern and touched my arm. Her expression asked what George's concern was.

I tried to mimic the lieutenant's actions, then pointed to my head to indicate that he was not in a good way. "No *wica...nagi*," I said in Lakota, indicating that he was not a whole man.

She nodded. "*Awent...*Morning Star *wasake*." She self-corrected her name, smiling as she said she was strong.

* * *

With US Army money in our hands, the five of us prepared to head back toward the Circled Cross Ranch. As we were about to rejoin the Oregon Trail, I spotted a wagon train off in the distance as it lumbered westward.

"Shall we wait for the wagon train?" Hap asked, though he said it as though already knowing the answer.

George simply shook his head. "Let's go," he declared. He knew, as did Dred and Hap, that the wagon train would spend a day resting near the fort. There was no point in delaying our return to the ranch. He also didn't say that wagon masters often resented visitors who might challenge their control.

We rode out with George in the lead, with me, Morning Star, Hap, and Dred riding side-by-side. It gave me a chance to work further on teaching her English and Comanche. I was sure George was quite entertained by my educating the woman I loved.

But for the beauty of the landscape and my work with Morning Star, we might have otherwise been bored to tears. The Oregon Trail was filled with stories left alongside the route by travelers. What was the tale behind a chest of drawers? A four-poster bed? A tiny grave? Not far off, the North Platte River meandered along. In a couple of months, it's waters would be frozen.

Now and then, George would fall back to chat. "One day, you will have to visit the fort and talk with the bartender at the sutler store. He can tell you how the famous mountain man, Jim Bridger, used to stop by and share wild stories of adventure with the local folks and troopers."

I noticed that Hap broke away from us and began riding point.

George saw my questioning look. "We're entering a part of the trail where Cheyenne occasionally make trouble," he said by way of reassurance.

With this new information lodged in my brain, it occurred to me that I hadn't taught Morning Star the rudiments of using the carbine. I took some solace in knowing that she was handy with the bow and arrow. I was determined to teach her to shoot when we got back to the ranch.

* * *

It was mid-afternoon when Morning Star reached out

with her hand on my arm and reined in her horse. I did likewise with Paint, as did the rest of our party.

"Cheyenne!" said Morning Star.

Of course, we saw nothing.

Hap came charging toward us and reined in his well-lathered horse. An arrow was stuck in the cantle of his saddle. "They're out there!" he exclaimed hoarsely, sweat dripping from his face. "Heathens nearly got me!"

I glanced at Morning Star, and she smiled back at me.

Our hands were filled with rifles. I made a quick scan of the area and spotted a bit of defensible high ground to our left among a stand of aspen.

"How many?" shouted George to Hap once his horse was under control.

"Couldn't tell," he said breathlessly. "Maybe they felt brave 'cause they thought I was alone," he added.

I shot a look up the trail and dug my heels into Paint's sides. He shot like a cannonball toward the trees. "There's at least five!" I shouted, swinging from my saddle and pointing to a band of warriors galloping our way. They likely thought they were chasing only Hap. They were in for a surprise.

Morning Star and the others charged right behind me into the trees. We dismounted, and the aspens were soon bristling with rifles.

"Over their heads!" ordered George.

The Cheyenne band was shocked by the sudden fusil-lade. George and I levered another round into our Spencers and fired again. The hostiles must have thought an army was holed up in the trees. Morning Star shot an arrow that stuck in a tree after narrowly missing the leader's head. He looked at what must have looked to be a strange arrow and shook his head. He'd never seen a Comanche arrow. Finally, their leader shouted an empty, face-saving cry, and turned tail with the others following behind.

We all looked at each other. It appeared as though we'd engaged them with no loss of life. "Looks like the good Lord was on our side," I announced.

"Good Lord?" questioned Morning Star.

"Wakan Tanka," I responded, with the Lakota name for the Great Spirit. "Lord...Watan Tanka...God." I shared. "God *wasake*," I added that God was strong.

"Appreciate yer Bible preachin', Isa, but we best keep an eye out fer them Injuns," advised Dred.

"Bible?" asked Morning Star. She was like a small child absorbing new words and new concepts. The Lakota were like my Comanche forebears in that most everything that breathed and a lot that didn't was some sort of spirit to be worshipped.

"Bible is book," I told her. "Is God's word, God's talk." I pulled my New Testament from my saddlebag to show her.

"Bible...God," she said, linking the two together.

I noticed George watching me approvingly. "Maybe, we ought to rest up a bit," he suggested. "Hosses could use a drink and a rest."

I grabbed my Spencer along with a handful of ammunition and guided Morning Star over to a nearby tree.

George, Dred, and Hap sat back to watch the show.

I set some pieces of wood atop a log about fifty feet from where I reckoned to have us shoot. Morning Star watched with unusual intensity.

I pointed out how to line up the sights at the muzzle and over the receiver, then proceeded to lever a round, taker aim, and blow a stick from the top of the log.

I started to hand her the Spencer. As she started to

place her finger over the trigger, I quickly dissuaded her of that. "Only when shoot," I cautioned.

Morning Star nodded and grasped the rifle.

George, Hap, and Dred ducked low as she waved the muzzle in their direction. Again, I cautioned her. Safety was critically important.

She looked off at the sticks remaining on the log, and I'd swear I detected a smile. She levered a round, aimed, and fired. A stick exploded from the log. She levered another round and repeated her achievement, then did it a third time.

George, Hap, Dred, and I dared not laugh.

Morning Star cleared the receiver and handed the Spencer back to me.

I gave her an appraising look, then walked over to the mule and fetched the spare rifle.

With the brief shooting lesson over, we wouldn't tarry much longer. I was looking at a herd of elk across the river, when Morning Star sidled up to me.

She pointed at the elk, smiled, and mimicked shooting the rifle.

I looked over at George. I didn't exactly feature hauling an elk carcass across the river, but he gave me a *why-not* shrug. It looked as though a couple of us were going to get wet. Since it was Morning Star's idea, I handed her my Spencer. It was a better firearm than the antique I'd given to her.

The elk herd was about a hundred yards off. It'd be a tough shot. Morning Star knelt by the river's edge and took careful aim. She chambered a round. Everyone held their breath with anticipation. She paused and raised the muzzle. "*Mato*," she said.

I'd heard that word among the Lakota. It meant *bear*. I stared at the elk. Sure enough, a momma silverback with two cubs was stalking an elk calf. Grizzlies were not to be messed with. Where there was a sow and cubs, there would be a boar around. The males were huge and could be nasty. I thought back on my own encounter and reflexively stroked my bear claw necklace. In any case, we wouldn't be dining on elk today. I nodded to Morning Star, and she handed the Spencer back to me.

We were soon mounted up and on the trail.

CHAPTER 15

WEDDING?

"Guess we'd better have a chat," said George as we sipped coffee on the gallery across the front of the house.

"About what?" I asked cluelessly.

He rolled his eyes. "Some things between men and women seem right natural, but there's more to it, Isa."

I looked over my shoulder through the window where Morning Star, Esmeralda, and Running Waters were busy making elk sausage. I could hear tidbits of their chatter. "Guess we better take a ride, George."

He nodded and smiled. "Let's do that."

We saddled up and rode out to a fishing spot overlooking the North Platte. It was a peaceful scene laid out before us. We wouldn't be fishing.

George sat, leaning his back against a tree. "In the second chapter of Genesis, God tells us, 'Therefore a man shall leave his father and his mother and hold fast to his wife, and they shall become one flesh.' Sounds simple, but that's just the beginning." He glanced at me to be sure I was taking this in. "There's more...plenty more. In First Corinthians, we're told that the husband should fulfill his marital duty to his wife, and likewise the wife to her husband. The wife does not have authority over her own body but yields it to her husband. In the same way, the husband does not have authority over his own body but yields it to his wife."

George had my attention.

"There's plenty more," advised George. "First Corinthians goes on to say that wives should submit themselves to their own husbands as they do to the Lord. For the husband is the head of the wife as Christ is the head of the church, his body, of which he is the Savior. As the church submits to Christ, so also wives should submit to their husbands in everything. Husbands must love their wives, just as Christ loved the church and gave himself up for her to make her holy, cleansing her by the washing with water through the word, and to present her to himself as a radiant church, without stain or wrinkle or any other blemish, but holy and blameless." The apostle Paul goes on to say that in this same way, husbands ought to love their wives as their own bodies. He who loves his wife loves himself."

Well, this was quite an earful. I shook my head in my naivete.

George laughed. "Don't worry. Running Waters is trying to share this with Morning Star. Her head is likely filled with what the Oglala Lakota women taught her. At least, you had the benefit of a real-life example with your folks."

"It's more than love?" I pondered.

"Commitment, faith, trust, respect, and more, Isa," George replied. "So long as those are your guideposts, you both will enjoy a wonderful marriage as blessed by God."

I threw a rock into the river and watched the ripples

in its aftermath quickly swept away by the current. "I suppose marriage can be like those ripples, if we lose all the Godly teachings that keep us together," I conjectured thoughtfully.

I laid a serious look on George. "What about the first night?"

He knew what I was referring to. "Just be gentle, Isa." That said, he looked back at the ranch house. I suppose we need to be building a place for you and Morning Star to live. My house and the bunkhouse won't do for newlyweds. Plus, winter's coming."

"Doesn't have to be much, George." I made the state-ment knowing that where we'd ultimately settle was undecided.

"There's one more thing, Isa." George gave me a dead-on stare.

"There's more?" I asked in an attempt to lighten the sudden shift in tone.

"What about your folks? You're nearly sixteen, and already a grown man by frontier standards." George wasn't letting me off the hook. "Shame your ma and pa aren't here to see you and Morning Star get hitched."

Talk about throwing ice-cold water on my dreams. Ma and Pa were a thousand miles away. Likely, they were hoping and praying that I was all right. What would my twin brother George, and Peter and Nadua think? I had set out on this vision quest, and I'd been led here to Wyoming. I'd met and fallen for a beautiful young woman barely as old as me. Could we wait? Should we? Oh, but these questions weighed heavily on my very soul.

George felt my consternation. "You might discuss this with Morning Star. If y'all are going to have a good life together, you must be able to share concerns." Then he chuckled and tossed a stone in the river. "Didn't your pa give old Buffalo Hump a passel of horses for your ma's hand?"

Consternation best described my thinking. How many horses would Spotted Elk want for Morning Star —assuming we could find him and he'd accept a half-breed son-in-law? "Dang it, George. You make sense," I said as my head swam with the possibilities God had thrown before me.

"God gave us the opportunity to make choices. It's up to us to decide the right ones.Consider waiting until spring. It'll give you time to write to your family and to decide where you want to settle." He paused, then smiled. "Unless you two are figuring to raise children while galivanting across the frontier."

I threw another rock into the river and another.

"No matter how many rocks you throw out there, the river is going to keep on flowing," George added with a hearty laugh. "Life goes on."

Well, I had my work cut out for me. I had to talk all this over with Morning Star. Given our mutual language challenges, it wasn't likely to be easy.

We headed back to the ranch house. Along the side, I thought on how I was inexperienced with women, at least as concerned affairs of the heart. I distracted myself by gazing about at the landscape and its bounty. This was a vast country with every sighting swallowed by its distance. There was a near-constant breeze at times, heralding changes in the weather. There were miles of grass and an endless web of snow-melt-fed streams. Trees grew taller and thicker alongside the creeks and rivers, and the grasses grew greener. Buffalo, deer, and elk grazed unbounded by man. Beaver had been nearly played out by the trappers, but were coming back. Scavengers like buzzards and coyotes prowled for carrion. There were mountain lion, bear, fox, bobcat, and…and wolf! "Where is Taabe?" I blurted. I realized that I hadn't seen him and his growing pack in several days.

We had almost reached the barn. "What did you say?" asked George.

"I haven't seen Taabe, Mua, or the pups," I replied.

"Saw them last night, Isa. He'll be there when you need him."

* * *

Morning Star was smiling as George and I strode in from the barn. The aroma of sweet baked bread hung in the air. I reckoned Running Waters had told her what George had gone off to talk with me about. I suppose that was a good thing, as it would avoid an awkward situation when I broached the subject of delaying our marriage. She dried her hands and walked over to me. She sure didn't look like any warrior woman at this moment, as she wore one of Running Waters's cotton frocks. It didn't stop me from enjoying a hug.

"*Sunkawaka?*" I asked in Lakota.

"Horse," she responded, with a laugh at knowing the word. Running Waters had been teaching her English.

I glanced over at the nearby table and saw that Morning Star and Esmeralda had been practicing printing words. Seeing a word on paper helped reinforce it. That having been said, I was pretty much resigned to living in a multilingual house. "We ride horses?" I asked.

Morning Star nodded. She pointed at the frock. "No dress," she said. "Change."

I nodded. The frock wouldn't do out on the ranch, and I had a particular place in mind.

* * *

Spotted Elk was concerned. He'd entrusted his daughter to Crazy Horse and the Oglala Lakota.

Chief Lone Horn listened carefully to his son's complaint. He had high hopes that the marriage of Morning Star to Buffalo Killer would cement peace between the Miniconjou and Oglala. "Tatanka Wiiyaska break promise to Awentia," observed the chief ruefully.

"Awentia run to *wasichus* Comanche," Spotted Elk said and nearly spat in disgust as he used the word for White man. He detested the Whites and knew nothing of the Comanche, so he resented Morning Star running off to a White Comanche.

Lone Horn shook his head. It wasn't the fault of the Oglala Lakota, and Spotted Elk's daughter was strong-willed. He counseled patience, hoping that she'd return to her people of her own free will. He wondered whether Crazy Horse knew the whereabouts of the half-breed boy?

* * *

Morning Star and I dismounted beside a cottonwood tree up from the north bank of the river. Canadian geese made a racket as they flew overhead, and a family of canvasback ducks nested in a protected embankment. Downriver, I spotted an eagle circling over the river to find a meal. A light mountain breeze lent a cool peacefulness to the scene. We ground-hitched the horses and spread a blanket upon which Morning Star laid out some bread and a bottle of fruit juice. It wasn't a grand picnic, but picnic it was.

We propped our carbines against the tree. They

served as an acknowledgment that we were still very much immersed in a dangerous frontier. Even a romantic setting demanded being on guard for trouble.

I kissed her, and she kissed me back. Oh, how I yearned for more. "I talk with George," I began.

Morning Star nodded, as though she knew what was coming.

"Isa *wiiyukta* Awentia. *WiiyakA* Awentia." In my halting Lakota, I told her I loved her and wanted to marry her.

She responded with a look that said love. She looked out over the North Platte, then turned to me with a smile and put her hand tenderly to my cheek. "Morning Star love Isa. Marry Isa."

Holy smoke! She was speaking English. "Marry in spring?" I asked lovingly. A bald eagle swooped down and snatched a fish. Having conquered my fear of broaching the timing of our marriage, I sort of felt like the eagle. Of course, Morning Star was not my meal.

Morning Star stared with deepest love into my eyes. "Spring flowers. Marry in spring," she cooed.

"My father and mother come. What of Spotted Elk?"

Her expression changed to one of concern at mention of her father. She hadn't thought of facing her father, or hadn't wanted to.

"Give horses?" I asked.

Her eyes brightened. "After marry?" She floated the idea out tentatively.

"We invite Spotted Elk?" Talk about an unsettled feeling.

"Invite?" she asked.

"Come to wedding," I said and signed that he would join the ceremony.

Morning Star didn't look so sure of that.

I stood and began carving *Awentia + Isa* in the bark of a tree. I carved a large heart around our names. It was a testament to our future together. I took her hand, and we walked to the water's edge. "Isa promise to you" I said firmly and lovingly. We kissed.

The hardest parts were ahead of us. My flesh had to stay strong, while we exercised patience. I had to get a letter out to my folks, and we needed to figure out a way to get a message to Spotted Elk. I was already considering reaching out to Buffalo Man.

I wrote a letter to my ma and pa and promised myself to pay a visit to Buffalo Man before the snows arrived. The letter was special, as I got Morning Star to print her name. I had her use her Lakota name, then wrote Morning Star beneath it in parentheses:

> *Dear Pa and Ma,*
> *Come to Circled Cross Ranch in the spring. I am marrying a Lakota woman.*
> *George and Running Waters send greetings and invite you to stay with them.*
> *Bring family.*
> *Your son,*
> *Isa*
> *Awentia*
> *(Morning Star)*

I folded it neatly and stuffed it in an envelope. The next step was to get it to Fort Laramie and in the mail.

Distraction now reared itself as critically important to us, waiting until spring to marry. Keeping busy kept our minds busy and diverted from succumbing to the passions of the heart. As George had counseled, this was about honor and respect.

* * *

A couple of days after my letter was posted, a courier arrived from Fort Laramie. Reining his horse in a cloud of dust, he demanded that he see me. No sooner had he placed the letter in my hands, then he turned and galloped off. Sometimes, the military way perplexed me.

It was too soon for my folks to have responded to my letter, yet the handwriting on the envelope was definitely in my pa's scrawl. I took out my Bowie knife and slit the envelope open. I nearly cut myself with excitement. Morning Star, George, just about everyone hung around, awaiting whatever news the letter shared. We didn't get mail very often, so this was a special occasion.

I took a deep breath and unfolded the letter. The ink had run in a couple of spots, but the writing was legible. I began to read:

> My Dear Son, Isa,
>
> With a heavy heart, we must tell you that your brother George was bit by a rattlesnake
> and did not survive the poison. We are all deeply saddened. He's buried with our family.
>
> We miss you and hope to see you soon. Maybe spring. Give our greetings to George and Running Waters.
>
> Love and blessings,
> Pa & Ma.

I was almost unable to finish reading. Tears began to flow. I couldn't hold them back. Dear God, why did you take my brother?

Morning Star felt my pain and clung to me. George placed a hand gently upon my shoulder. The pain was brutal. The news hit me like a bear's paw swatted against my head. The anguish was excruciating.

I had now borne witness to both George and my pa losing children. Yes, I understood the often-harsh laws of the frontier. Life was fragile. The country was demanding of man and beast and took many before their time. Yet, I had faith that while God might take loved ones away, he also gave us others to love. George and Running Waters had found baby Zebediah. My folks would add Morning Star to our family. As to family and God, it wasn't about taking and giving, it was about enduring love.

* * *

September was sliding into October. We talked about the wisdom of Morning Star and me visiting Spotted Elk. We dared not be caught in the early throws of winter, yet the longer we waited, the greater the likelihood of the Miniconjou Lakota being unaccepting of a partially White boy marrying a Lakota maiden. We nevertheless procrastinated.

When we weren't helping with chores and language lessons, Morning Star and I explored the region around the Circled Cross Ranch. We weren't sure as to where we might ultimately settle and make a life, but sought a site to build a small cabin until a decision might be made. Would we stay here in the northern plains or move to Texas, and my roots?

George was building a good-sized herd. He'd brought in a couple of Herefords and was trying to breed them with the longhorns. The breeds didn't exactly get along at first, but he'd begun to have some success. As an O'Toole, raising cattle ran in my veins. The longhorn and Hereford crossbreed had an appeal for me that I began to take seriously. The Herefords were great foragers, produced outstanding beef quality, and were adaptable to their surroundings, while the longhorns were hearty, calved easily, and were disease resistant.

I shared my ruminations about ranching with Morning Star.

"No hunt buffalo? No fight Cheyenne?" she asked. Much as she had taken to the ranch, her thinking was still muddled with Lakota warriors roaming the mountains and plains as they hunted and fought.

I reckoned that we would be fighting Indians for some time to come. As to hunting buffalo, I didn't see Morning Star and me hunting buffalo for sustenance or making clothes, implements, or even teepees. "We hunt," I assured her. "We fight," I said with a wry smile. We'd surely be dealing with threats, as the Whites encroached over tribal lands. The Fort Laramie Treaty of 1868 was already a shambles.

Chapter 16

Unwelcome Visitors

We finally settled on a spot in the far northwest corner of George's spread. He gifted the land to us, figuring that, were we ever to leave, it could serve as a retreat for him and Running Waters. With occasional help from Dred, Hap, and George, I managed to construct an adequate log cabin roughly twelve feet square. We installed a beat-up stove I'd found alongside the Oregon Trail. We dug the obligatory privy and built a small shack over top. Come spring, we'd worry about a well. Come to think of it, the cabin wouldn't be occupied until after the wedding. It would stand for now to taunt Morning Star's and my human desires. Dear Lord, give us strength.

By the time the cabin was finished, hints of winter were blowing our way. Leaves began transitioning to brilliant reds, yellows, and oranges. Bears prepared to hunker down for the winter. Ever-heavier frosts lent jeweled crowns to the grasses each morning. The cold waters of the North Platte River turned ever more frigid.

Buffalo robes and heavier coats became the fashion of the day.

* * *

I was walking across from the house to the bunkhouse, absentmindedly watching my breath form clouds in front of me, when I nearly met full on with a Lakota pony. I looked up to see none other than Buffalo Man. Four warriors accompanied him. They appeared peaceful enough, though they were fully decked out for trouble were it to come. I noticed one riderless pony, and that should have given me a hint as to what was to come.

Buffalo Man jumped from his saddle and extended his hand. He was a might shorter than me, but was of a muscular build with handsome facial features.

This was a good start for a visit, or so I hoped.

"*Wowahwa kola*, Tathanka," I said as a welcome. I offered peace and friendship.

"*Awentia?*" he asked.

My thoughts instantly turned to the possibility that he'd come for her.

Morning Star appeared on the gallery of the ranch house. A buffalo robe was draped over her shoulders. "*Hau, mitákuye oyás'e*," she called out a welcome.

Buffalo Man motioned her to come.

I found myself standing speechless as some sort of drama began to unfold before me.

"Wičhóunta Elk." He invoked the name of Morning Star's father and motioned her to come with him.

Morning Star shook her head. "*WiiyakA* Isa," she said firmly. "Wičhóunta Elk come here," she said and mixed in English, but drove home the point that her father should come to the Circled Cross Ranch. She and Buffalo Man rattled off some Lakota words that were too fast for me to follow or translate. The upshot was that she was staying with me and we'd be married in the spring.

Buffalo Man looked none too pleased. He looked at me.

I smiled. "Isa *wiiyukta* Awentia. *WiiyakA*." My words in the frosty air made it crystal clear that I loved her, and that we would marry.

The Lakota warrior looked sternly at Morning Star. He had been sent by Crazy Horse to fetch her back, so she could be promised to another warrior. "Tasunke Witko *wiiyAza*," he stated firmly that Crazy Horse would be unhappy.

About this time, Taabe, Mua, and their now nearly full-grown offspring appeared. It was as though I had a wolfpack backing me. It was strong *sunipu* for Comanche and had to have the same effect on the Lakota. Silence reigned. We seemed to be at a stalemate.

Morning Star stubbornly resisted, and I was standing by her.

Buffalo Man gazed at me and the wolves. He must have been asking himself what sort of powers I must possess. As he shook his head and was about to say something, an arrow struck one of the Lakota.

Morning Star and I were initially startled. We then saw what Buffalo Man had yet to turn and see. A band of perhaps twenty Cheyenne hostiles were approaching the ranch with guns and bows and arrows already in play. We raced to the ranch house with Buffalo Man and his warriors right behind us. George and Running Waters were nearly bolled over as we crashed in through the front door. "Cheyenne!" I shouted.

Rifles were quickly distributed and windows manned. Dred and Hap were in the bunkhouse and heard the commotion. The bad news was that they were stuck there, but the good news was that we could lay down a crossfire on the attackers. I was so glad that my Spencer was in good working order and that Morning Star could use a rifle. We didn't have enough for all of our Lakota allies, but we did the best we could. The wounded Lakota warrior wasn't in fighting shape, anyway, as Running Waters worked to extract the arrow from his back.

The yard was swarming with the shouts and whoops of the Cheyenne, as they poured arrows and bullets at us. However, their boldness was costing them. One savage, intending to set the roof afire with a torch, was blown from his pony by a bullet from Morning Star. I kept levering bullets into the receiver of the Spencer and aiming and squeezing the trigger as fast as I could. The carbine got smoking hot right quickly.

Dred and Hap were laying down fire from the bunkhouse. At least six Cheyenne hostiles lay dead or dying, and a couple were still on their ponies but wounded. They were paying an extraordinarily high price for their aggression. With a yell and sweep of his war lance, the leader called off the attack and beat a retreat.

Silence followed, but for the moans of the dying.

We stood looking at each other. Ten of us, sweating and panting from the anxious excitement of but moments before. George began to laugh. It served to ease the tension.

"Coffee?" asked Running Waters. Tin cups appeared as if from nowhere. Guns were stored away after being reloaded.

Esmeralda brought out a platter stacked with bear sign. Buffalo Man and his band looked at the baked treats, saw me begin to enjoy one, and descended on them. A handful of languages floated about. Dred and Hap ran in from the bunkhouse to join the celebration.

Buffalo Man grasped my hand firmly and smiled. "Isa *wiiyukta* Awentia. *WiiyakA*." He looked over at Morning Star, as she talked in a friendly way with his warriors. "Tasunke Witko?" He shrugged, as though Crazy Horse would simply have to get over it. My Lakota friend had acknowledged the inevitableness surrounding Morning Star and me.

"Better check outside," I said as I donned my hat. It had occurred to me that a couple of the Cheyenne were in bad shape, and two ponies had fallen. I checked the load in my Colt revolver.

George, Morning Star, and Buffalo Man followed me outside.

We counted five dead warriors. One had just breathed his last, and a sixth barely clung to life. I mercy-killed the two wounded ponies.

Taabe was dragging one of the dead Cheyenne away. Sadly, I shrugged it off. The savage had tried to kill us.

Buffalo Man pointed to the remaining Cheyenne who'd gathered to the north about a half mile away. He signed to me and George to let them retrieve their dead warriors. I knew that it was the honorable thing to do. The Lakota, along with Hap and Dred, emerged from the house and helped us drag the bodies of the dead to a spot about a hundred yards north of the barn. It was obvious that the Lakota wanted scalps, but it was Morning Star who stepped up and dissuaded them. My faith teachings were beginning to have an effect on my betrothed.

The wounded Cheyenne warrior looked as though he

might survive, so we carried him out to lie with his brothers. With a caring smile, Running Waters placed a cup of coffee and a bear sign beside him. But for the seriousness of the occasion, we'd have enjoyed a hearty laugh. I hoped his brothers got to him before Taaba and Mua. In fact, I was concerned that my wolf companion had carried off human prey.

I waved at the Cheyenne, and their leader waved back. We'd all live another day—whether at peace or war remained to be seen.

One thing led to another, and Buffalo Man and his band were soon enjoying a dinner with us. I hoped and prayed today's allies would not become tomorrow's enemies. The alliances on the frontier were known to be quite fickle. Buffalo Man and I were developing a friendship not unlike the one my pa had with my Comanche uncle Spirit Talker.

Buffalo Man said that he would pass on our invitation to Spotted Elk to come to our marriage in the spring. He explained that part of the Lakota marriage ceremony involved the symbolism of the bow and arrow to illustrate life balance. The bow was useless without the arrow. But the bow and arrow are more than about togetherness, for the arrow must fly true to its target, and the bow that sends it must be strong. One is worthless without the other, and thus a balance must be achieved. Buffalo Man looked off thoughtfully at the setting sun and signed that it was important to have balance between man and woman.

I asked Buffalo Man to tell Spotted Elk that we'd be honored for him to share the bow and arrow story at our wedding. We agreed that this might ease the father's concerns. It would also give me time to come up with a

gift to compensate him for giving up his daughter to me.
I had something special in mind.

Morning Star had been listening in rapt attention to
the conversation between Buffalo Man and me. I think
she was impressed with the way Buffalo Man and I were
able to talk, that former enemies had become friends.
She smiled admiringly at me. "Isa strong *sunipu*," she
said, using a mix of English and Comanche. She reached
under the table for my hand and squeezed it lovingly.
"Tomorrow, we hunt," she said. "No bear," she added
with a little laugh at her own humor.

I was confident that Morning Star would make a
great hunting companion. It seemed that George and
Running Waters' advice was making sense. My Lakota
maiden and I had been caught up in the initial throws of
attraction and love and were now on a path toward truly
knowing each other as friends, partners, and companions built upon mutual trust, honor, and respect. It didn't
hurt that she was beautiful to look upon, and somehow,
she was attracted to me. I'd never thought of myself as
handsome, but she apparently thought so.

CHAPTER 17

A HUNT

We awakened to find Buffalo Man and his band gone, including the wounded warrior. As Morning Star and I strolled out to the barn to saddle horses for our hunt, I couldn't help but look out to where we'd laid the bodies of the Cheyenne warriors killed in the fight against us. They were gone—the wounded foe as well. Morning Star and I smiled knowingly at each other. The dead would be given honorable funerals. Most Whites would not have thought to honor enemy dead, but we were confident that the Cheyenne would not forget our respect for them.

George advised us at breakfast to hunt within the boundaries of the ranch, as he was concerned that the Cheyenne might yet be lingering. He had also rounded up a lever-action Henry rifle for Morning Star and given it a special cleaning. It was a 1873 model, and it caused me a touch of envy, even though my .56 caliber Spencer held a bit more power. I had seen the Henrys among Custer's Seventh Cavalry troopers, but never held one. Now, I could see it close up.

As to ranch boundaries, our best estimate was that his spread encompassed around seventy or eighty thousand acres, so staying on the ranch boundaries wouldn't restrict us at all. Most everything south of the North Platte and west of Fort Laramie was land comprising the Circled Cross Ranch.

Paint snorted and whinnied to fully display his anxiousness to be ridden, and we chose a chestnut mare for Morning Star. There was a nip in the air, so we wore full buckskins and tied buffalo skin blankets behind our saddles. Importantly, we wore moccasins, as I didn't want the jingle of spurs messing up and stalking. Running Waters gave us some elk jerky to snack on, so that went into my saddlebags. We supplemented bota bags of water with a couple of Army canteens George had acquired.

We mounted up, waving to George and Running Waters as we headed westward. I had a place in mind where we could find elk, if not buffalo.

* * *

About a half mile out, Taabe appeared. He trotted up to us, so I reined in and slipped from my saddle. He came up to me and nuzzled my hand. Apparently, he was choosy about which humans he ate. I motioned Morning Star to dismount, and the three of us enjoyed a hug fest. Whatever had caused Taabe to take the Cheyenne warrior would remain unknown, as he wasn't talking. I gathered that he, Mua, and their two offspring must have been especially hungry.

Taabe got his fill of loving, then turned and took off ahead of us. We mounted up and followed. Mua and the rest of their pack joined Taabe on the hunt. He led us about two hours out to the top of a hill where there was a break in a stand of aspen. From that vantage point, the vista before us was incredibly beautiful. The vastness of the rolling hills broken by valleys carved out by the weather and the meandering Laramie River was breathtaking. Importantly, there was a herd of elk to our right, moving toward the river and about a hundred buffalo grazing to our left.

"Buffalo? Elk?" I asked Morning Star.

Taabe and Mua had already moved toward the elk, as they had elk calves in their sights.

"Buffalo, *tathanka*," responded Morning Star.

A male buffalo might weigh as much as twenty-five hundred pounds and stand six feet or more at the shoulder. The cows were not nearly so big, but might still weigh a hefty fifteen hundred pounds. Of course, a momma buffalo protecting her calf could spell trouble. Assuming we would enjoy a successful hunt, we faced the task of hauling our trophy back to George's house.

We followed a path that led us through a natural divide between two grass-covered hills. This enabled us to approach the buffalo unseen. We were downwind from most of them. I had it in mind to bag a young bull. He'd still be a load to haul home, but I was disinclined to shoot a cow or calf this time of year.

I had already decided that the kill shot would be Morning Star's. I signed that we be silent. We dismounted and ground-hitched our horses. "You shoot." I let my beloved know that the kill shot would be hers.

Morning Star smiled and squeezed my arm appreciatively.

We snuck silently up the steep hill to our left, as I reckoned it would give us the best view of the buffalo. I led the way.

As I neared the crest of the hill, I froze, causing Morning Star to nearly bump into me. I turned with finger to lips. I'd peered over the top of the hill to find myself looking at the backside of a mountain lion. The lion had apparently decided that buffalo calf would make a delicious meal. "*Igmuwatogla*," I whispered the word for mountain lion in the Lakota tongue.

Morning Star's eyes grew wide, and we both back-tracked down the hillside. Even with the power in our guns, there was really no point in interrupting the lion's hunt. To kill the beast would have been senseless, as he wasn't hunting us.

Soon enough, we heard the thunder of buffalo on the run, as the mountain lion stirred himself up a bundle of trouble in chasing a buffalo calf. The adults didn't take too kindly to his intentions. I was glad that we were in the valley, as all the action was above us and we were protected by the terrain. Or so we thought.

We had nearly made it back to our mounts when there was a tumbling, screaming, and scraping sound followed by a loud thud behind us. A young buffalo had fallen down the steep incline. He lay stunned, and it was obvious that he'd broken a foreleg. He was going nowhere. I nudged Morning Star to shoot the poor beast. He was facing us. "Shoot above his legs," I advised.

Morning Star nodded. She chambered a round, took careful aim, and put a bullet into the buffalo's heart and lung area. Mercifully, he died quickly.

My ears still ringing from the close proximity of Morning Star's rifle shot, I leaned my rifle against a stump. I took out my knife and began to walk toward the buffalo.

Morning Star was beaming from her successful

shooting and began to place her Henry beside my Spencer.

Well, that old mountain lion had failed to bag a calf but had seen the young bull plummet over the hilltop. I peered over the buffalo carcass to find myself staring head-on into a pair of yellow eyes and an angry hissing beast behind them. His tail twitched, as he sized up his menu. Given a choice of fight or flight, I reckoned hunger drove his choice. He was clearly of a mind to protect what he saw as his meal.

While I was engaged in a stare down, Morning Star overcame her own initial shock and fear. She slowly brought the Henry to firing position. "Don't move," she whispered in perfect English.

I wasn't about to make any move that would cause that cat to leap.

The explosion from the muzzle of Morning Star's rifle about deafened me in the close confines of the little valley. I felt the heat of the bullet as it sailed past my ear, but her shot caught the mountain lion between the eyes. He collapsed where he'd stood ready to spring at me.

I took a deep breath and turned to Morning Star. She dropped the rifle and ran to me with tears in her eyes. She buried her face in my chest with huge sobs. I loved the softer side of my warrior woman.

After a few moments, we pulled back. "We have much work," I said. Indeed, we'd be skinning two beasts and packing quite a bit of meat. I decided that I'd take the mountain lion's claws to fashion a necklace for my woman. She'd certainly earned it.

As we went to work on the buffalo and mountain lion, Taabe appeared with his pack. We would share our kill.

* * *

Field dressing, skinning, and cutting out meat was the easy part of what lay ahead of us. The temperature was cool and the skies clear, as we worked as speedily and diligently as we could. Taabe's family was overjoyed with their feast, as I trimmed out choice buffalo haunch for them. Unsurprisingly, they all stayed clear of the mountain lion corpse. Only Taabe was brave enough to take a sniff. I suppose there was a certain professional courtesy among predators of the wild.

I cut out and collected the claws from the mountain lion, then had an idea and turned to Morning Star. "*Igmuwatogla* for *ate*," I suggested. "Mountain lion for Wičhóunta Elk."

She thought a minute, then smiled and nodded approval.

We made short work of skinning both lion and buffalo.

While Morning Star began packing our hunting treasures, I managed to find and fell a couple of juniper saplings. It didn't take long to fashion a travois. By the time we had everything together, it was getting on to mid-afternoon. With only two horses, we'd ride double on Paint and rig the travois to the mare. It'd be slower going, but I calculated that we'd make it back to George's house a bit before sunset. We might even have buffalo steaks for dinner. We'd have quite a story to tell, as we savored the fruits of our labors.

As I thought on our hunt during the ride home, it came to me that it wasn't a hunt in the traditional sense. It had been more a case of prey falling almost literally into our laps and us seizing the opportunity. The seizing the opportunity part seemed a metaphorical commentary on life. If the buffalo hadn't fallen into our laps, followed by the mountain lion, we'd still be looking for prey.

* * *

Esmeralda was first to see us coming and rushed to the new iron triangle chime hanging on a gallery hook used to announce the approach of guests. The thing pealed its message out loud and clear. George, Running Waters, Hap, and Dred all came running to see what was happening.

George looked bust-a-button proud to see us riding across the pasture, and we were soon in their midst. It was obvious that they all were impressed with our apparent hunting prowess.

They were all smiles as we pulled up. I eased Morning Star down from behind me and then got down from the saddle myself.

Running Waters looked from me to Morning Star and back, then gave an approving nod to George. I reckoned she was judging that we had not fully consummated our love while out hunting. "We eat buffalo tonight!" she announced.

CHAPTER 18

WINTER COMES

Joy struck when a letter from my folks arrived toward the end of October. They were still dealing with the loss of my twin brother, but would head up here to attend our wedding, which we planned for the end of April. I figured that they'd dodge the worst of any lingering winter weather.

We had yet to hear from Spotted Elk. I felt that the invitation to participate in our wedding would smooth over any ill feelings. Also, Morning Star and I decided to gift him with a tunic made from the tanned skin of the mountain lion she'd killed.

"We have not heard from Tathanka or your father, Wičhóunta Elk," I observed at breakfast one frigid morning. Despite the warmth of the kitchen, I felt chilled. The hot coffee helped, but I dreamed of cuddling with Morning Star for warmth.

"Patience," she counseled.

Running Waters nodded agreement with Morning Star and placed plates heaped with eggs, bacon, and biscuits before George and me. "The way of the Red man is not always quick," she advised me.

Nevertheless, I found myself worried.

The days were growing ever shorter as we greeted November. The temperature hovered at freezing or below, especially at higher elevations. Having spent several seasons here near the Laramie Mountains, George was convinced that the winter would be a brutal one and was pleased that we'd constructed another storm baffle to help protect livestock from the elements.

We laid out the ropes from house to bunkhouse and bunkhouse to barn. As I'd already personally experienced, these were handy during near-blinding blizzards. I shared their purpose with Morning Star, and she shared how a couple of young Lakota boys had frozen to death in a winter storm. She fully understood and appreciated the ropes.

Morning Star and I hunted together frequently. Once, our stalking some deer put ourselves dangerously close to a Crow encampment. That we had gotten so near without detection was more a testament to icy cold weather that kept the warriors inside, enjoying the warmth of their teepees. Also, a light snow had fallen, perhaps a harbinger of George's fears.

* * *

We didn't have turkeys roaming around Wyoming, so there was no feasting on the birds at Thanksgiving, however, we all chowed down on buffalo, elk, and deer and sang our hearts out. I even banged out tunes on the piano while Dred strummed the banjo and Hap blended in with his harmonica. As usual, George promised to eventually tune the piano. Morning Star caught the celebratory fever and was soon singing along. She was amazed at the music, as that of her people did not offer quite so much variety. She was fascinated with Dred's banjo, but sat by my side at the piano at times banging keys in an attempt to join in.

The meal ended with all of us gathered around the hearth and George reading from the Bible and sharing the story of the first Thanksgiving. As the sun dropped toward the horizon, everyone was already asleep. I was overjoyed, as Morning Star fell asleep beside me. Feeling her warmth sent me off to dreams of spring and our becoming man and wife.

* * *

Spotted Elk stood on the rocky rampart overlooking the empty Oregon Trail and thought on what he'd heard from Buffalo Man. The Miniconjou were still on good terms with the Oglala, though it didn't appear that their alliance would be cemented with marriage any time soon. He was reluctantly impressed with what he'd learned of me, the half-White and half-Comanche who saved his daughter from the Crow and fought Cheyenne to protect her. I seemed unlike other Whites whom he'd encountered. That I, as a young suitor, wanted him to share the tale of the bow and arrow at my marriage to his daughter, lifted his heart. Despite his simmering rage at the onslaught of the Whites with their diseases and soldiers, he found himself inclined to accept the circumstances and proudly give Morning Star to me. The wedding was five moons off.

Meanwhile, the wagon trains wouldn't be risking the trail through the big mountains with the risk of violent snowstorms. The invasion of Whites was abated for now.

* * *

To say that winter hit with a vengeance would be to grossly understate its fury. The first blizzard struck in mid-December. Threatening dark clouds gathering in the northern sky, gave sufficient warning to move live-stock to the storm baffles and load in extra hay and feed. We might not be able to protect the beasts from the bitter cold, but they'd be sheltered from the arctic blasts.

I'd awakened just before sunrise to a relentless howling wind that drove icy snow against the bunkhouse. Had I been unfamiliar with the strength of the bunkhouse walls, I'd have feared it being beaten down and filled with snow. We'd had the foresight to store plenty of firewood in a sheltered bin just outside a bunkhouse side door, so we stayed toasty warm.

Dred passed the time practicing on his banjo while Hap plaited new straps for a worn halter. I cleaned my Spencer carbine and Colt revolver a few times over and honed my Bowie knife to a fine edge. While I sorely missed Morning Star's company, we had plenty of food. Among the three of us, we could whip up edible meals. Oh, and there was plenty of coffee.

I recalled that it was in one of these storms last year that George and Running Waters found the Lakota baby they'd adopted. I also dared not forget the time I followed the wrong rope through the blinding snow and wound up in the barn instead of the ranch house.

With December and despite the storms, the Freeman family was focused on preparing for Christmas. To that end, I worked at putting together a mountain lion claw necklace for Morning Star. I'd bartered for some silver beads to Fort Laramie, so I interspersed the beads between the claws. By my decidedly male judgment, the gift was perfect for a warrior woman—*my* warrior woman. I found a beautiful piece of aspen wood and carved a cross to serve as the centerpiece at the front of the necklace.

The true test of the fierceness of any storm was where Taabe and his pack sheltered. The hunting was right-poor during and immediately following blizzards. The four wolves either took refuge near one of the baffles or begged their way into the bunkhouse. Sleeping with warm, living, breathing wolves sure topped blankets. They were even friendly with Dred and Hap. Importantly, they seemed to sense that the livestock was not prey.

I found myself deeply appreciating the interludes between storms, as they afforded me the opportunity to dine with Morning Star. When she wasn't helping Running Waters and Esmeralda with chores, she busied herself fashioning a tunic from the mountain lion pelt and adding decorative beadwork. It would make a spectacular gift for her father, Spotted Elk.

* * *

It wasn't long before we found ourselves steeped in the doldrums that entailed day-to-day living in the snowbound wilds of the frontier. We replenished firewood, checked on the livestock, and did whatever we could to stave off boredom and prepare for the first blushes of spring. Soon enough, the woods and prairies would be teeming with wildlife, and that would mean that Indians hunting parties would be roaming about, and the

Oregon Trail would once again be laden with wagon trains.

We did learn that Lieutenant Colonel Custer was planning another expedition, this time to a place called the Black Hills. Rumor had it that Custer was to seek out appropriate locations for a fort and to investigate the potential for mining gold. George was especially concerned about gold mining, as its discovery would surely bring the demise of the Red man.

One morning in early March, George and I took a ride out to where we'd constructed the little one-room log cabin that was to serve as the first home for Morning Star and me. We approached cautiously. From the outside, it appeared to have weathered the winter quite well.

We dismounted and ground-hitched our horses. Paint was on high alert, and I observed Taabe and his pack keeping a goodly distance away. "Something's wrong, George," I whispered. "I feel it." We took our carbines with us.

Approaching the front door, I noticed that it was a tad cockeyed, and a hinge was broken. George and I got the same idea simultaneously and moved to either side of the door. We listened. I heard a snorting sound and some scratching, as though someone or something was moving in its sleep. I kicked the door hard, and it swung open with a bang. A roar came from inside. We reflexively stood back to either side of the door, as a grizzly rumbled out the door. He was none too happy. Worse, his sow had apparently departed without him. He didn't even look our way, as he lumbered by close enough to feel his hot breath. The old silverback headed toward the nearby creek.

Now, I'd faced a grizzly before, and there was the

incident with the mountain lion, but I praised God that the bear hadn't taken offense at us, awakening from his winter slumber.

We peeked inside the cabin. Reckoning the bears to be gone, we went about performing what repairs we could. The bears had enjoyed the foodstuffs we'd stored away, so they would have to be replenished. The door hinge repair was easy enough.

"You think they'll be back, George?"

"Running Waters says she learned from a Lakota woman that they used pine needles to discourage bears. Seems that the critters find the pine sap odor offensive." George paused in thought. "There are a few junipers behind the cabin. They have a sweet odor like pine. Let's rub juniper needles against the walls and especially outside. That ought to repel the bears."

I reckoned it was worth trying. I sure didn't figure on bringing my bride back to a cabin full of bears. We would rub the place down and return in a couple of weeks to be absolutely certain our bear repellent worked.

* * *

I reckoned to get in a hunt before winter ended and spring kicked in. After hunkering down indoors for much of the winter, we'd begun to feel like the hibernating bears. Of course, we weren't sleeping nearly so much as the grizzlies. Bringing home some elk or deer meat would give us a break from our diet of beef and bacon.

There had been a couple of breaks in winter's wrath. We called them *thaws*, but the term was loosely applied to mean the difference between freezing and subfreezing. Freezing meant that we could get out to hunt nearby, as we dared not venture too far, given how fickle winter tended to be. The thaw meant we were able to go out and bring home meat from cattle that hadn't made it to George's storm baffle. Combined with stored vegetables and fruits, we did eat quite well through the winter.

Morning Star and I did pretty much everything together, much to George's and Running Waters's amusement. They were convinced it would change once we married and my Lakota wife would fall into the roles of mother and homemaker. We'd see.

My plan was to venture up to the Oregon Trail and hunt the woods between the trail and the North Platte. It was near midday, when we ventured out. We were dressed warmly against the morning chill, as we ventured out. We soon found ourselves looking out over the ice-choked river. There was a raw beauty to the scene laid out before us. Beaver had already gone to work shoring up their home on a creek that ran into the river, and a few birds braved the cold. I pulled up and dismounted, motioning to Morning Star to do the same. Something on the opposite side of the river had caught my eye, then disappeared. I glanced over at Taabe. His ears were alert, and his nose was sniffing the breeze wafting across the river. "Something moved," I whispered to Morning Star and pointed to a stand of cottonwood. "I feel danger."

Whoever or whatever was not likely to cross the icy waters unless they meant to attack. The river ran a bit deeper where we were, so crossing meant breaking ice and handling a horse with water to its neck.

We walked our horses downstream a way. There was no point in engaging the apparent threat. I looked down and spotted fresh deer tracks in the snow. There were five deer, so far as I could make out. We stalked the deer while cautiously looking across the river sporadically.

We ground-hitched Paint and Morning Star's mare and headed on foot, now sensing that our prey was near. I saw an intersecting track and squatted. Just as I dropped, I heard an explosion from across the river. A bullet whizzed past me and grazed Morning Star's arm. She dove to the ground beside me. Had I been standing, I'd likely have been killed.

"Hotamo'e!" came a shout from the north riverbank.

I peeked above the berm to see a warrior shaking his fist at me.

"Name mean Bull Elk. He, Cheyenne," explained Morning Star as she saw her blood reddening the snow under her.

We were now hunkered behind this protective berm. It was risky, but we could poke our heads above to catch sight of our attacker. I tore off my bandana and wrapped Morning Star's arm tightly. Another bullet whizzed over our heads. I had my Spencer in hand, but was reluctant to appear above the berm. There'd be little or no time to properly aim.

"Hotamo'e kill Whites!" hollered our attacker. Bull Elk apparently knew some English.

I'd had enough of Bull Elk. I handed my hat to Morning Star. "You poke my hat up when I signal."

She nodded with a smile. She'd figured what I was up to.

I belly-crawled my way about twenty feet downstream. Staying prone, I poked my Spencer between a couple of dead branches lying in front of me. I levered a round into the chamber and pointed my carbine toward the area we'd last seen our attacker. I nodded to Morning Star, and she poked my hat above the berm.

I caught the reflection of the sun from a rifle barrel across the river and aimed slightly behind it. I squeezed off a round simultaneously with Bull Elk. My hat went flying, but so did the Cheyenne. Silence filled the air.

I gazed hard at where Bull Elk had stood.

Morning Star gave me a quizzical look.

Suddenly, Bull Elk appeared. He waved madly with what remained of his rifle. He whooped and shouted with all sorts of false bravado. It seemed that my slug had blown his rifle stock away at the grip. It had bloodied Bull Elk's hand and ruined the rifle. He was too far off from me to see, but he likely took some splinters in his chest and face.

I stood and waved friendly-like. My gesture served to anger him more. As a final expression of his anger and hatred, he shook his fist at us before stalking off.

Morning Star and I stood and looked at each other before coming together in a relieved hug. "That was close," I said, stating the obvious. Then I looked down at the bloodied bandana wrapped around her leg. "Let me see," I said.

She sat and permitted me to undo the bandana and examine the wound. It needed tending to, but not with what we had out here.

I rewrapped it and helped her stand. "We'd better go back," I advised.

She looked up at me, shook her head, and smiled. "We team. We hunt."

I kissed her. "We hunt," I repeated, though I felt it ill-advised.

I looked back down at the deer tracks. With all the fuss, I'd forgotten about the intersecting prints. They were paws. From the size, I figured them to be from a bobcat.

Taabe hadn't forgotten the paw prints. While he'd surely get the better of the cat in a squabble, he'd just as soon not engage. While bobcats were not of the prowess of mountain lions or bears, they could put up a nasty fight. Taabe would likely win, but he'd take a terrible clawing in the melee.

Morning Star fell in behind me, though we moved slowly due to her wound.

With Taabe keeping an eye out for the bobcat, we could focus on the deer. About fifty yards up the trail, we came to a spot where the deer had leaped away. The shots from Bull Elk and my rifles likely frightened them away.

We laughed, as we both sighed and shrugged resignedly. "Hunt over?" she asked.

Just then, Taabe growled. I glanced up. The bobcat was sitting on a tree limb about twenty feet above us and another twenty feet downstream. I felt as though he was smiling at us. But the cat was no threat. Besides, I couldn't kill an animal just for the kill. I had to admit that his fur would look great on Morning Star. "Let's go home," I urged.

"Come on, Taabe." My wolf companion looked long-ingly at the bobcat, but fell in behind us as we walked back to our horses.

I mounted Paint and looked lovingly at the Lakota maiden beside me. My, but she was beautiful and such a wonderful complement to me. "We have wedding to get ready for," I said.

"I think my father come," she predicted.

I sure hoped so. The last thing we needed was to have her father displeased. I boosted her gently into her saddle.

CHAPTER 19

THE WEDDING

I was walking from the barn to the house, as Running Waters had invited me to join them for a midday meal. I'd ridden out with Dred and Hap on the south pasture earlier and rescued a longhorn cow from a bog. It had been a challenge to haul her bulk from the mire, as it tended to suck her in place. She likely weighed around a thousand pounds, so it took the three of us working together with ropes to free her. After she was out, we had to coax her away from the bog. These cattle could be downright dumb at times.

Anyway, there I was headed to chow down and enjoy some time with Morning Star, when the jingle of a harness caught my ears. I looked in the direction of the noise. Lo and behold, it was my family. Pa and Ma were seated at the front of the wagon. Trailing behind on horseback were my brother Peter and Nadua, followed by Shorty and Hardy driving about fifty longhorns.

"Morning Star, come out!" I hollered. "My family's here!"

I waited for her to run to my side before heading

toward the arriving entourage. George, Running Waters, and Esmeralda came running out to join the welcoming committee. Even Hap and Dred emerged from the barn.

Pa pulled up a way off from the house for fear of running over someone. He jumped from the wagon and helped Ma down.

I was running so hard that I nearly ran into them. Poor Morning Star was barely able to keep her legs under her, as I half-dragged her along. "Ma! Pa!" We hugged. I pulled Morning Star into the family hug, as Peter and Nadua quickly joined in.

I stepped back. "Pa, Ma, this is Awentia," I said, in an attempt to formally introduce Morning Star.

Ma took her hands and pulled Morning Star into a hug. Ma's Comanche eyes shone with love.

George and the others arrived on the scene. Pa and George began to shake hands but then hugged. It had been a very long time since they'd last seen each other.

Hap stepped up and began to lead the wagon team toward the house while everyone walked alongside, engaged in the chaos of greetings. Aside from the big event, the next weeks would be filled with all manner of stories. George's fireside chats would catch breaths of new life.

With the arrival of my family, we now awaited the arrival of Spotted Elk. Would he make it in time?

"We brought y'all a wedding gift," said Pa with a nod to the small herd of longhorns. He had it in mind to make me into a rancher.

* * *

A pair of dark eyes watched the arrival of my family from a distant stand of junipers. Hatred oozed from him with every breath. It was none other than Bull Elk. He not only hated the Whites but now held a grudge against me. He figured there'd be an opportunity to take my scalp and perhaps kidnap the beautiful Lakota woman.

He figured the Oglala Lakota wouldn't be around to help defend against an attack next time, nor will I get off a lucky shot that disabled his prized rifle.

* * *

The next several days saw a whirlwind of activity. There was an incredible amount of catching up to do. There was much that letters had been simply inadequate to communicate. My ma and Morning Star seemed more like sisters than mother and soon-to-be daughter-in-law. English, Comanche, and Lakota filled the air around them.

George and I shepherded my pa and Peter around the Circled Cross Ranch, as so many improvements had been made since my pa's last visit. Pa was quite impressed with the storm baffles and how they'd helped the livestock endure the harsh winter.

On the third day after their arrival, we rode out to the little cabin where Morning Star and I would begin our lives together. We brought a few supplies as part of the effort to restock the place from the hibernating bears. As we approached, I noted that the door was slightly ajar. I thought I'd closed it last time I was here.

Pa dismounted and walked up to the front door. "What's that stink?" he asked.

"Juniper," I responded. "It keeps the bears away."

"Shucks. It'd keep me away, too," Pa said with a laugh. He turned and laid a serious look on me. "You've come a long way, son. Your vision quest has taken you down a very special trail." He opened the cabin door and peeked inside. A playful squealing sort of cry greeted him. "Oh my!" he exclaimed and stepped back.

We all froze.

"Looks like mama and papa griz like the smell of juniper," Pa laughed, but with a touch of concern.

We mounted up quickly and grabbed our rifles, for as the cubs came bounding from the cabin, their mother appeared not fifty yards away. She reared upright with all of her six feet height and maybe four hundred pounds and gave us what for. The cubs ran to her, and she gave them a scolding and tumble while chasing them out of danger.

"Where's that doggone silverback?" I hollered while scanning the area for that big boar we'd seen just a few weeks back. I'd thought the beast would have been put off by the smells of humans and juniper. I'd been wrong.

We didn't have to wait long. The big grizzly had decided that my cabin was his territory and returned with an angry baring of fangs and a roar that would awaken the dead. I'd swear he stood upright at close to nine feet.

Despite the threat, I sure wasn't of a mind to kill him. If it was to be him or us, so be it. Was there another way?

Taabe appeared from around the side of the cabin with Mua and the now nearly full-grown pups. Four big timber wolves were a sight to behold, especially with an angry bear before them. It'd be one whale of a battle. I'd heard that in battles between wolves and grizzlies, the wolves often held their own, or the beasts even backed off without fighting.

A possible solution to the standoff came to my brain, and I figured it was worth a try. I looked at George and my pa. "Shoot over the bear's head." I hoped to scare him off. With the noise and threat from the wolves, the bear just might leave. We were about to try to make my cabin the least desirable place on earth for the grizzlies.

We fired multiple rounds into the air, and Taabe and his pack growled and made feints toward the grizzly. With a snort and growl, the big boar dropped to all fours and lumbered off behind his sow and cubs.

"Hold fire," I shouted. "I think Mr. Grizzly is about done with this place."

Pa and George looked at me with prideful smiles. I had taken charge of a difficult situation.

"Good job, son," offered my pa.

We headed back to the house.

$$* * *$$

The planned date for the wedding way only three days away. Would Spotted Elk arrive in time? Would we wait? Could we?

George was primed to conduct the ceremony, and I had told him about the Lakota bow and arrow tradition. We were as ready as we could be.

It occurred to me that I hadn't seen Morning Star's dress. I asked Running Waters about it. But she wouldn't say. I even tried to bribe Esmeralda with sweets to no avail.

George had taken me to the sutler store at Fort Laramie and bought me some new pants with red suspenders and a dark-blue shirt. I decided that I'd wear my beaded moccasins, as my boots were pretty much worn out.

Far as I could tell, we were ready.

Two evenings before the planned day, a column of about a dozen Lakota came into view riding in from the western pasture. Crazy Horse led the way, followed by Buffalo Man and an older man whom I figured to be Spotted Elk. Imagine having the mighty Chief Crazy Horse as a guest at my wedding!

The column stopped alongside the barn. Crazy Horse stared at me and then at my pa. A look of recognition swept across his face. "Pohya Isa!" he declared and slid from his pony to greet my pa.

"Tasunke Witko," replied Pa.

Buffalo Man helped Spotted Elk from his pony. Morning Star's father apparently suffered from the wounds of past battles and hunts. He proudly limped forward and held his hand out to me. "Isa O'Toole *wowahwa kola*," he said, by way of welcoming me to his family. It was clear that he'd made peace within his soul as to the fate of his daughter.

Morning Star saw her father from the gallery in front of the house and came running. "*Apé*," she called and flew into his arms.

"Welcome Tasunke Witko, Tathanka, Wičhóunta Elk," I said by way of greeting. "*Ana o'a hi'it*, I said, using the Comanche tongue to invite them to dine with us. It was aimed at making them feel welcome.

We were involved with greetings when George motioned for us to come to the other side of the barn. He led us over and unveiled a special surprise for our guests. He'd constructed a large lean-to sufficient to house the entire Lakota delegation.

The expression on Crazy Horse's face was one of great gratitude at George's thoughtfulness. The Indians were not fond of being cooped up within four walls, so the lean-to was well-appreciated.

Crazy Horse grasped George's hand in gratitude and smiled with genuine warmth. This was how it was supposed to be between the people, regardless of skin color. George's hospitality was deeply appreciated.

Running Waters appeared on the gallery and rang the iron triangle. That got everyone's attention. There was no space inside the house for the better than twenty guests we'd assembled, so the evening meal would be served in the bunkhouse, where beds had been pushed aside and makeshift tables set up.

"Sun go," I said and signed to describe the sun setting. "*Ana o'a hi'the it*," I said, now repeating my welcome, but this time as an invitation to eat. Esmeralda, bless her heart, had already added to the stew that was cooking on the stove. Running Waters and Morning Star quickly worked toward adding to the feast. It was a prodigious task to add food for an additional dozen people, but they were up to it. No one went hungry around the Freeman home.

* * *

After dinner, I visited with Spotted Elk. He told me how grateful he was that I'd saved his daughter from the Crow and then protected her from Buffalo Killer. He'd learned from Crazy Horse that I was a grandson of the great Comanche Chief Buffalo Hump, and it seemed to impress him that I descended from a strong bloodline. He'd also heard of the exploits and strong medicine of Pohya Isa.

I had a special gift for Spotted Elk that I'd managed to keep as a secret from Morning Star. Dred and Hap had helped me. Spotted Elk's eyes went wide when I led a handsome Appaloosa stallion from the back of the barn and handed him the reins. He'd shaken my hand when we first met. Now, he hugged me. "Is good," he said, in shaky English. "Awentia and Isa wiiyakA," he declared. He officially approved of our marriage.

I left him standing there with his arms wrapped around the Appaloosa's neck.

* * *

The big day finally arrived. My stomach was a tad unsettled, so I passed on breakfast. Hap and Dred spent the morning in the bunkhouse teasing me about the wild hoedown music they reckoned to play.

I peeked outside and was relieved to see a clear, crystal-blue sky. The weather looked to be perfect.

I hadn't seen Morning Star all morning, and I wasn't permitted in the house. I yearned to be with her. George and Pa gave me knowing looks wherever they could. Even Buffalo Man gave me a wink.

At noon, Esmeralda stepped out onto the gallery. She was done up beautifully in a pink satin dress with her hair falling in ringlets over her shoulders. She stepped up to the iron triangle and then threw herself into ringing it as loudly as she could. It belied her ladylike appearance. Importantly, it began the process of everyone gathering.

Hap and Dred sat on the gallery playing the harmonica and banjo respectively, while our guests sat about on makeshift seats.

I stood nervously beside a flower-draped archway under which we'd be wed. My brother Peter stood by my side. He seemed about as nervous as I was. I'd been far less nervous facing wild animals. Ma and Pa sat on a bench behind me while Crazy Horse and Buffalo Man sat opposite them.

George stepped from the house and gave a speech to

welcome the guests. Spotted Elk stood with him. I was surprised to see that he wore the mountain lion shirt that Morning Star had made for him. I wondered at how she'd managed to get the gift to him without me knowing. Then again, there had been a lot of secretive stuff going on.

George raised his hands to silence everyone, and Hap began to play a song that sounded like some sort of march.

I saw George gaze off beyond me, so I turned to see Running Waters slowly leading Morning Star toward me. Oh my, but my bride appeared as a gift from God. To describe her as beautiful would fall far short of the truth. Her white buckskin dress, white moccasins, and hair woven with white lilies set off by a purity and joy of spirit that gave her a glow that put the sun to shame.

She was soon standing before me, her eyes locked on mine.

George droned through some words I'd never remember about vows and love and respect. All the guests looked to be hungry, so I'll give him credit for only taking a few minutes. Upon completing his message, he turned to Spotted Elk and motioned him forward.

Spotted Elk did a masterful job with a mix of sign, English, and Lakota in explaining the bringing together of the bow and arrow as being akin to the importance of balance in a marriage and in life. He delivered it with great grace that left everyone silent for a few moments after he'd finished. Spotted Elk ended the ceremony by giving me a bow and Morning Star an arrow. We nocked the arrow in the bowstring and together fired the arrow off into the distance. We turned to see tears of pride in the old warrior's eyes.

George pronounced us husband and wife. "You can kiss her now, Isa," he whispered.

I swept Morning Star into my arms and gave her a kiss never to be forgotten.

We lingered in our embrace for a few moments before I turned and invited everyone to celebrate with music and feasting. The bunkhouse had never before witnessed such a party.

Crazy Horse came over to me and grasped my shoulders. "Isa *kola* Tasunke Witko," he said solemnly. He'd declared me to be his friend.

"*Kola*," I replied with the same commitment. "*Kola wasake*," I said as I emphasized that our friendship was strong.

In my peripheral vision, I caught George watching me and nodding approval. Apparently, I'd just made a great advance in relations with the Lakota.

I'd taught Morning Star a dance my pa and ma used to do, so I took advantage to swirl her about in my arms. No wonder Pa liked it.

The celebration wore on, and everyone ate their fill. Finally, George asked Dred and Hap to stop the music. "It's time for Isa and Awentia to leave us and begin their life together," he announced, with a booming voice that likely shook the surrounding mountains.

We were ushered outside where Paint and a beautiful chestnut mare were saddled. The mare was draped with flowers, while Paint seemed to look at her disdainfully. He was a man's horse, not to be decorated with pretty flowers. We said our goodbyes, mounted up, and headed for the cabin. The place was finally going to be used for what it had been intended. As we rode side by side, sharing loving looks, I hoped the bears had not returned.

* * *

Reining in at the cabin, I dismounted and helped Morning Star from her saddle. I recalled something my pa had said about carrying her across the threshold. Morning Star stepped to me, expecting a kiss, but I swept her off her feet and carried her to the front door. I flipped the latch with a free hand and stepped on through with a laughing wife in my arms. A bed beckoned from across the room.

There were no bears. We didn't care about the juniper smell. Paint and the mare grazed happily.

Chapter 20

Bull Elk Returns

We had not quite finished digging the well, but it was an easy walk to fetch water from the North Platte River. There were still plenty of ice shards and a strong current fed by snowmelt. Morning Star quickly set up house-keeping, and I went about watching over the beeves Pa had gifted us with.

"Isa rancher?" asked Morning Star over coffee after about a week of routines neither of us were especially attuned to.

I shook my head. "No," I shared. "I could be, but is that our life?" In a sense, my pa had perhaps unwittingly placed his ranching life upon us.

"Hunt…ride…love," said Morning Star reflectively. It was clear that she was of a mind to have our little cabin serve as a home base while we roamed the land seeking adventures and satisfying our passions. The downside was that it was a life that wouldn't earn us a living.

I had shared my faith with her. Reinforced by George and Running Waters, she had come to a faith in God and was learning about Christ. Despite me being only a year older, I was far more mature in the ways of the White man's version of life. I could live off the land. In fact, I had during my travels from Texas. If ranching wasn't for us, what might our future be? Was my vision quest not ended?

For now, we had plenty of food and no worries about the near future. We'd eventually have to make decisions.

May slid into June. The snowmelt-fed river still sparkled each day in the morning sun. Our life together seemed made in God's heaven. The woman I'd first seen months back as a prisoner in Crazy Horse's encampment and then fallen in love with, completed me as a man. I was but a month from turning sixteen years old, yet was a full-fledged man by any measure.

* * *

We awakened in late morning to the sounds of birds raising all sorts of alarms. I slipped on my clothes and stepped outside. Morning Star followed close behind. We scanned the landscape. Taabe and his pack were standing guard and on full alert. Paint and the chestnut mare were prancing about in the corral with all manner of whinnies and snorts. Something out there was stirring them up. Taabe led his pack off as though intending to investigate.

I wondered whether the bears had decided to return. The juniper smell had mostly faded away.

Morning Star and I looked at each other and shrugged. We turned to head back inside. Just as I followed her through the doorway, an arrow buried itself in the wood beside my head. The thud and accompanying vibration were true attention-getters. As I stepped over the threshold, a second arrow whizzed past my head and hit the far interior wall of the cabin.

Morning Star and I stared at it. "Cheyenne!" we said simultaneously.

"Hotamo'e kill!" came a not far off cry.

I praised God that his aim with a bow was as poor as it had been with a rifle.

I peeked out from the cabin window. A spiral of smoke arose from the other side of a hill, only a hundred feet or so from our front door.

Bull Elk saw me and released another arrow. It thudded harmlessly into the window frame.

We were safe for the moment, but wouldn't be going out the front door. I took my Spencer from the spot where it rested above the fireplace. Morning Star fetched her Henry rifle. It appeared that we'd be in for a siege, but we needed to let Bull Elk know that we wouldn't be easy pickings.

I sighted the Spencer at a gun port we'd had the wisdom to drill into the door. I didn't poke it through, as I didn't want Bull Elk to see it. I waited patiently for his head to appear above the crest of the hill he was hiding behind. What I saw next was more than concerning. Four Cheyenne warriors stood beside Bull Elk. So, he had brought together his own band.

They must have sensed that I was waiting for them, because they ducked behind the berm. Every now and then, we could see eyes peer above the hill, but they were not making themselves targets.

We expected Hap and Dred to bring supplies in a couple of days, but we seemed to be stuck for the present.

Bull Elk's patience apparently began to wear thin. Indians generally did not like sieges, and he was no exception. He strode to the top of the berm with his four companions. "Hotamo'e kill!" he shouted.

I reckoned it was time for action. I aimed the Spencer and squeezed off a shot. The blast about blew out our ears in the confined space of our cabin, but one of the Cheyenne caught my bullet in his arm and toppled back. I levered another round into the receiver and fired. I missed, but the Cheyenne dove back to cover. I figured they wouldn't be poking their heads above the berm again for a while.

"What we do?" asked Morning Star.

I shook my head. "We wait until dark," I responded. I had a trick up my sleeve unless Bull Elk did something unexpected before then. A part of me resented the Cheyenne's interruption of our wedded bliss.

* * *

Morning Star brewed some coffee.

I had taken a few sips when it occurred to me that our privy was outside. We wouldn't be using it so long as Bull Elk held us at bay. We had plenty of food, but not more than a day's supply of water. And no indoor privy! Our situation didn't look especially encouraging.

I wondered what had become of Taabe? What was on his wolf heart? With five hostiles out there, he was likely hesitant to attack.

Every now and then, Bull Elk sent an arrow at the cabin as a reminder of his presence.

Me? I decided to not waste ammunition. I had a sense that Bull Elk was also waiting. What might he be up to?

Morning Star and I were struggling to patiently await darkness. There'd be no moon visible this night, so we might be able to escape.

What was on the mind of that rogue Cheyenne? Maybe, they were also waiting for the night.

The sun soon completed its descent behind the mountain beyond our cabin. Darkness slowly enveloped the landscape, though we could still see a glow from Bull Elk's fire. The stars were mostly hidden behind clouds, thus adding to the virtual blackout.

We snuffed out the one candle in the cabin and plunged ourselves into total darkness. We'd now move about by feel. We waited while our eyes adjusted to the lack of light. Once outside, the partially hidden stars would offer us just enough light.

If Bull Elk was watching, the darkness in our cabin surely signaled to him that we were up to something. Turned out he was the one who acted first. He lofted a burning arrow into the cabin roof.

EPILOGUE

The American western frontier was mostly unforgiving, a meeting of savagery and civilization. By 1873, ever more towns were springing up. They served as bell-wethers to the civilizing of the frontier. *The Wolf's Quest: Isa's Adventure Begins* offers a peek into the courage, faith, endurance, and pure grit entailed in the conquest of the West. I decided at age fifteen that it was time to venture out on my own. Little did I know that the Great Plains Indian Wars loomed ahead.

Life expectancy on the frontier was nothing like today. A male Indian did well to live beyond age thirty, and women could expect to live a tad less. Little wonder that older tribesmen were highly respected. Life expectancy for Whites wasn't much better. A White man on the frontier tended not to live beyond his late thirties. Notably, the brevity of life generally meant that folks had to mature sooner. By the time a man or woman reached age fifteen or sixteen, he or she was pretty much an adult in terms of others expecting him or her to carry an adult set of responsibilities.

Dangers? Anthropology-minded folks claim there were as many as thirteen distinct tribes of Comanche from the Quahadi or *antelope eaters* in the north to the Penateka or *honey eaters* in the south. Mix in Kiowa, Apache, and Tonkawa, and settlers had their hands full. The very name Comanche loosely translates in the Ute tribal language as *kumantsi* or *enemy*. Capture by the Comanche invariably led to terrible outcomes. A fearsome lot these tribes were. The horse, coupled with a long history of trade for the latest weapons and farm-grown foods in and around the Comancheria, produced a highly aggressive nomadic culture heavily dependent on the buffalo. For example, Penateka Comanche Chief Buffalo Hump led more than 600 warriors on a raid through the heart of Texas in August 1840, murdering Texans, looting the city of Victoria, and looting and burning Linnville on their march to the Gulf of Mexico. It was not until 1858 that Texas Ranger John Salmon *Rip* Ford led the force of 102 heavily armed Texas Rangers and 100 Indian allies that brought the Comanche to their knees at the Battle of Little Robe Creek on the Canadian River in Oklahoma, as depicted in a previous Frontier Chronicle *Warpath: Jack's Faith is Tested.*

The northwestern plains were peopled by many tribes, but especially the Sioux, comprised of three groups: Dakota, Nakota, and Lakota. The Lakota were made up of seven subgroups: Oglalas (famed for Red Cloud and Crazy Horse), Hunkpapas (famed for Sitting Bull), Miniconjous, Oohenunpas (Two Kettles), Itazipa-colas (Sans Arcs), Brulés (Burnt Thighs), and Sihasapas (Blackfeet). The Lakota history was no less combative than Comanche or Cheyenne. Despite the violence of the frontier, it's notable that the Lakota held to a worthy set of virtues, especially generosity, courage, fortitude, and wisdom. The North Platte country referred to in *The Wolf's Quest: Isa's Adventure Begins* was part of the Wyoming Territory established in 1868.

Oh, I do refer to bison as buffalo. Just for the record, bison and buffalo are quite different. Visualize the water buffalo and then the shaggy, awkward bulk of the American bison. Seems that *buffalo* came into common usage in America to refer to the bison, so I've chosen to use buffalo in my writings. Notable too is that the evasive four-legged critter many unwary folks refer to as an antelope is properly called a pronghorn.

Historically notable in the Wolf's Tales is that the longest and most used cattle trail was the Great Western Trail from 1874 to 1893. It ran from Matamoros, Mexico, to Val Marie, Canada. As many as three hundred thousand cattle each year would eventually be driven up that Great Western Trail.

I enjoyed no modern creature comforts. The invention of telephones was decades into the future. Transportation? Horses, mules, and oxen—ridden or pulling wagons—were the vehicles of choice. I enjoyed having no refrigerator to preserve sweet treats. There were no flush toilets or showers. Folks mostly ate what grazed upon or grew from the land. Learning was squeezed from the few books that might be found, especially the Holy Bible. Can't say as the living of the era was luxurious unless you counted the sheer grandeur of majestic landscapes and of nights so quiet you could hear the stars twinkling. To fully appreciate the place, you simply had to love the incredible beauty of the outdoors. Fishing the meandering Guadalupe River in Texas or the chill waters of Wyoming's North Platte River, hunting deer and pronghorn, raising cattle and horses, and reaping the bounteous yield of the rich soil was sheer joy for a courageous visionary few. For a teen on the frontier, life could be pretty good…mostly. Otherwise, it was downright dangerous.

Thus far, I was quickly growing to manhood. My vision quest was leading me on a path known only to God. I was striving to conquer personal fears and prejudices, fight Indians and bandits, defend against wild beasts, travel the wild country, drive cattle, find the love of my life, and endure a search for a life purpose. As you have seen, I especially draw upon my faith and what I was taught by my parents. And yet, all of this is constantly tested. I had to learn to trust in instincts forged from my biblical and life lessons. Yes, I'm on a frontier adventure and more. And you, dear reader, will now be able to follow me, Isa O'Toole, as I seek my own way in life and share my adventures. May God ever bless me and Morning Star.

GLOSSARY

Bear sign—Cowboy slang for donuts.

Big Father or Great Father—All-powerful Indian deity.

Bota bag—A canteen fashioned from leather and popular among Indians, mountain men, and many travelers of the western frontier.

Cold Camp—Camp without a campfire, generally done to avoid the smoke that might alert threats.

Dog run—The sheltered space or breezeway between two sections of some southern ranch houses. Living quarters were usually on one side and sleeping quarters on the other.

Fletch—The fin-shaped bird feathers on an arrow that help stabilize its flight.

Gallery—A synonym for porch. Folks in the West often called the structures across the front of their homes galleries.

Life debt—A cultural phenomenon in which someone

whose life is saved or spared by another becomes indebted or in some way connected to their savior.

Pemmican—Lean dried strips of meat pounded into a paste, mixed with fat and berries, and then pressed into small cakes.

Possibles bag (aka parfleche)—A leather or canvas sack carried by cowboys and containing essentials like soap, matches, bandages, extra spurs, smoke makings, and playing cards

Remuda—A herd of horses frequently deployed on trail drives and by Plains Indians.

Rendezvous—Annual celebratory gathering of mountain men.

Sand—Courage.

Shaman—Medicine man.

Teepee—An enclosed conical transportable shelter constructed of long poles and buffalo hides with a vent at the top to permit smoke to escape.

Travois—A wedge-shaped structure constructed of two poles and a cross-beam lashed together and dragged behind horses, mules, or dogs by Plains Indians.

COMANCHE TRANSLATIONS

Aitu—Not good

  Ana o'a hi'it—Phrase for *desire to eat*

  Ap—Father

  Aruka—Deer

  Eetu—Bow

  Ekakwitsubaitu—Lightning

  Ekapitu—Red

  Eekasahpana paraiboo—Army officer (soldier chief)

  Haa—Yes

Hawokatu—Hollow, loose

Hoikwa—Hunt, look for prey

Isa—Wolf

Isa wasu—Poison

Kaahaniitu—deceive, cheat

Kahni—Life

Kamakuna—Loved one

Kee—No

Kobe—Wild horse

Kohto—Build a fire

Kooitu—Die

Kuhmabai—Married

Kuisa—Coyote

Kuuna—Fire

Kuya akatu—Afraid of

Kwakuru—Defeat someone

Kwihnai—Eagle

Mua—Moon

Mukue—Spirit

Nahuu—Knife

Natsuitu—Strong

Numu—Cow, Cattle

Numunahkahnis—Family

Numunuu—Referring to the members of the Comanche tribes. Literally: people.

Ohapitu—Yellow

Onaa—Son or daughter

Paa—Water

Pabi—Friend

Paaka—Arrow

Peeka—Kill

Pia—Mother

Pia huutsuu—Bald eagle

Pia wa'óo—Comanche words for mountain lion, puma, or cougar.

Pihi—Heart

Pohya (or poya)—Walk

Puuka—Horse

Sunipu—Medicine (as in *strong medicine*)

Suumaru—Ten

Taa Narumi—Master; God

Taabe—Sun

Tabu—Coward

Tamu—Rabbit

Tasiwoo—Buffalo

Tenahpu—Man

Tomoobi—Sky

Tosa—White man or woman

Tosaabitu—White

Tumah tuyai—After life

Tuhibitu—Black

Tumhyokenu—Believe, trust

Tu Taiboo—Black man

Umaru—Rain

Unha haksi nahniaka—Phrase for *what's your name?*

Wa'ipu—Woman

Wasápe—Bear

Wutsutsuki—Rattlesnake

LAKOTA TRANSLATIONS

Ate—Father

Ayústan—Abandon, retreat, leave

Enákiya—Stop

Hau, mitákuye oyás'e—Welcome

Igmuwatogla—Mountain lion

Isan—Knife

Iya Tate—Wind

Iyaya—Go, leave

Jiji—Light hair

Katá—Kill

Kola—Friend (male)

Kize—Fight

Maka—The earth and grandmother of all things

Mas'óphiye—Trade or barter

Mato—Bear

Mini—Water

Nagi—The spirit that has never been a man

Nanji—Jealous

Niya—Ghost

Okin—Pretty

Oyate—The people or nation

Sapa—Black

Ska—White

Scan—Sky

Sunkawaka—Horse

Sunkmanitu tanka—Wolf

Takuwe—Why

Tanka—Wolf

Tatanka—The great beast (patron of health, ceremonies, provision)

Unk—Created by Maka; embodies all evil beings

Unktehi—One who kills

Wakan Tanka—God (monotheistic)

Wamaka nagi—Animal spirit

Wanbli—Eagle

Wani—Four winds (weather)

Wasake—Strong

Wash tay—Good

Wasichus—White man

Wasna—Pemmican

Wi—The sun (chief of all gods)
Wica—Complete man
Wicasa—Man (gender)
Wicasa wakan—Shaman
Wiiya—Danger
WiiyakA—Marry
Wiiyuka—Coward
Wiiyukta—Love
Winyan—Woman
Wowahwa—Peace
Zuzeca—Snake

THANK YOU

Thank you for taking the time to read *The Wolf's Quest: Isa's Adventure Begins.* If you enjoyed it, please consider telling your friends or posting a short review. Word of mouth is an author's best friend and much appreciated.

Thank you.
Mark Greathouse

WATCH FOR: THE FRONTIER CALLS: TWO SOULS, ONE ADVENTURE
(THE WOLF'S TALES 2)

In *The Frontier Calls: Two Souls, One Adventure*, the second volume in the *Wolf's Tales* series, seventeen-year-old Isa O'Toole rides deeper into the untamed West...where survival demands more than grit, and faith is the only compass that never fails.

Having begun his vision quest in the shadow of bloodshed and doubt, Isa—half White, half Comanche—now faces a harsher frontier. With his Lakota wife Awentia, a loyal wolf, and his one-man pony, Isa is no longer just seeking purpose...he's living it, one perilous step at a time.

But the frontier doesn't forgive weakness. Ambushed by Arapaho warriors, stalked by grizzlies, and caught in the rising flames of the Plains Indian Wars, Isa must battle not only enemies on horseback but the ghosts within—memories of past killings and the weight of a destiny he's still learning to bear.

As friendships deepen and dangers close in, Isa realizes his calling reaches far beyond himself. The answer to his vision quest lies not in revenge or mere survival, but in forging peace between clashing worlds and building a future grounded in faith, family, and the land.

Can Isa lead others toward harmony in a land built on division? Or will the price of peace be more than one young man can carry?

AVAILABLE FEBRUARY 2026

Acknowledgments

Authoring books doesn't simply happen in a vacuum. The author provides the creative talent and crafts the stories, but there's so much more that demands acknowledgment. There are lots of folks and places that contribute to my authoring endeavors. So it is with *The Wolf's Quest: Isa's Adventure Begins.* The tale is set in 1873 and transitions to 1874, sharing the trials and tribulations of a young man forced to meet the challenges inherent in the dangerous vastness of the western frontier. But this novel stands apart. At its core, it is also about the taming of that frontier. The protagonist epitomizes the freedom of America's western frontier and represents a final bastion of honor in America. This tale follows Jack O'Toole's earlier Frontier Chronicles series, beginning with his adventures in *Perilous Trails: Jack's Adventure Begins.* Hopefully, readers will find the Wolf's Tales series beginning with *The Wolf's Quest: Isa's Adventure Begins* worthy of their time and emotional involvement. Saddle up and ride into the future with Jack's oldest son, Isa.

I've been blessed with many friends and family who have supported my writings. My wife Carolyn's reviews and encouragement were a huge help, along with very important tech support from our sons Mike and Matt. Thanks to my nephew Shawn and pastor Randy for their faith insights. Many more friends and family have contributed support at some level to the creation and publication of my Wolf's Tales, be it encouragement or advice.

Naturally, I am major grateful to the great folks at the Wise Wolf Books imprint of Wolfpack Publishing. The team they bring to publishing is first-rate in editing, cover design, and the myriad tasks that lead to successful book sales.

It's only right to acknowledge my ancestors who were actual settlers of the South Texas frontier. In addition to inspiring me, they provided a quite helpful true-to-life framework as to the life and times on the Texas Nueces Strip. It has been appropriate to weave them into the tapestry of my Western novels. Matthew Dunn (1815-1855) immigrated to Corpus Christi from County Kildare in 1845, established a homestead on Upriver Road, and served as a sutler to General Zachary Taylor's Army in the Mexican-American War. Peter Dunn (1807-1890) immigrated from Ireland in 1850 and established a blacksmith shop in Corpus Christi; John Dunn (1803-1889), my great great-great-grandfather, raised cattle and grew thousands of acres of cotton; Lawrence Dunn (1837-1864) fought and died with Captain Ware's Confederate cavalry; and my great-great-grandfather Nicholas Dunn (1835-1912) was a rancher, drover, livestock speculator, and Comanche fighter of some repute. My cousin John Beamond *Red John* Dunn (1851-1940) served as a Texas Ranger in the 1870s under Captain Bland Chamberlain (Company H), subsequently joined a *vigilance committee*, became a farmer and merchant, and curated a museum of military weapons displayed to this day in the Corpus Christi Museum of Science & History. Red John Dunn's brother, Matthew Dunn, also served as a Texas Ranger, and another cousin, Rut Evans, served as a Texas Ranger in the 1890s (Company E, Frontier

Battalion, Alice, TX). My cousin Patrick Dunn was quite successful at raising longhorns on North Padre Island, just east of Corpus Christi, from 1883 to 1937. John Hillard Dunn (1883-1958), whose personal narrative about his family and his own adventures inspired my pursuit of my Texas family legacy, drove my own writings. Finally, my grandfather, Horace Charles Greathouse, served as a Texas Ranger in 1920 (Company C, Austin, TX). Such real-life characters, coupled with actual events, have served to reinforce the historical settings for my writings. I've also personally walked the very landscapes traversed by my fictional and historical characters.

Most of my authoring has occurred in my office as decorated to channel my inner Texan, but my creative juices have often been inspired and imagination stoked in cafés and coffee houses across America. My favorites were Hester's Café & Coffee Bar in Corpus Christi, TX; Nueces Café in Robstown, TX; Java Ranch Espresso Bar & Café in Fredericksburg, TX; PAX Coffee & Goods in Kerrville, TX; Ragged Edge Coffee House and Bantam Coffee Roasters in Gettysburg, PA; 1889 Coffee House in Helena, MT; Dunn Brothers Coffee in Rapid City, SD; Postmasters Coffee & Bakery and Brio Coffeehouse in Waynesboro, PA; Birdie's Café and American Ice Co Café in Westminster, MD; Deja Brew Coffee House, New Oxford and Deja Brew at Miney Branch, Carroll Valley, PA; Baltimore Coffee & Tea Co., Frederick Coffee Company & Café, and Dublin Roasters in Frederick, MD; Qualle Café and Grounded Coffee & Bakery, Cherokee, NC; Palace Café, Amarillo, TX; and Unto Others Café, Lamar, CO. I must admit to also frequenting a few Dunkin Donuts and Starbucks around our fine nation. The décors and easy listening music in these fine establishments combined with savory cups of coffee tended to set me in the right creative frame of mind. They also afforded engagement with many fine citizens of our nation.

Last but not least, I'm especially thankful for the many folks who have read and enjoyed my books.

I do believe it's important to acknowledge how the Old West represents the brave pioneering spirit of settlers who met the challenges and transcended mere survival to enable America to achieve exceptional growth. The settling of the American frontier west is replete with tales of leveraging freedom for individual achievement. I hope you'll agree that reliving our past— even through history-based fiction—often has the effect of pointing the way to an ever-brighter future. Might we be up to it? I hope that the inspiration I've drawn from my having walked the very earth my characters have trodden, coupled with my extensive historical research, will enable readers to fully experience the grit, adventure, and passion of my characters while sensing aromas of gunsmoke, trail dust, leather, and bluebonnets.

Thanks kindly to all of you, and please do enjoy *The Wolf's Quest: Isa's Adventure Begins.*

About the Author

Award-winning author Mark Greathouse's love for the western genre draws upon his deep family roots and love of the outdoors honed from teen years hiking the Appalachian Trail and family travels across America's frontier. Greathouse began writing full time after a successful career as a business executive and later as an entrepreneurial investor and advisor. His service as president of several business and community nonprofits led to their extraordinary growth. He holds a BA in English and MBA in marketing. Greathouse donates time and books annually to support wounded military warriors.

A member of Western Writers of America and the Wild West History Association, he also contributes articles on the history of America's west to western-themed magazines. Greathouse was recognized as a 2024 Finalist in western genre by the American Literary Book Awards for his sixth Tumbleweed Saga, *Nueces Truth: Texans Face War's Realities.*

His *Frontier Chronicles,* a series of western novels aimed at adventure-minded teens and young adults while weaving a Christian message within their fabric, are aimed at lighting fires of truth, faith, hope, and life purpose in the bellies of today's teen boys and girls. Just as seeds must be sown to reap the harvest, so the seeds of faith must be planted to raise tomorrow's men and women.